THE CRISSCROSS SHADOW

The HARDY BOYS *Mystery Stories*

BY FRANKLIN W. DIXON

THE TOWER TREASURE

THE HOUSE ON THE CLIFF

THE SECRET OF THE OLD MILL

THE MISSING CHUMS

HUNTING FOR HIDDEN GOLD

THE SHORE ROAD MYSTERY

THE SECRET OF THE CAVES

THE MYSTERY OF CABIN ISLAND

THE GREAT AIRPORT MYSTERY

WHAT HAPPENED AT MIDNIGHT

WHILE THE CLOCK TICKED

FOOTPRINTS UNDER THE WINDOW

THE MARK ON THE DOOR

THE HIDDEN HARBOR MYSTERY

THE SINISTER SIGN POST

A FIGURE IN HIDING

THE SECRET WARNING

THE TWISTED CLAW

THE DISAPPEARING FLOOR

THE MYSTERY OF THE FLYING EXPRESS

THE CLUE OF THE BROKEN BLADE

THE FLICKERING TORCH MYSTERY

THE MELTED COINS

THE SHORT-WAVE MYSTERY

THE SECRET PANEL

THE PHANTOM FREIGHTER

THE SECRET OF SKULL MOUNTAIN

THE SIGN OF THE CROOKED ARROW

THE SECRET OF THE LOST TUNNEL

THE WAILING SIREN MYSTERY

THE SECRET OF WILDCAT SWAMP

THE CRISSCROSS SHADOW

"Come on, Joe, the wagon's here," Bert cried out.

"Come on, Joe. He mustn't get away!" Frank cried.

Hardy Boys Mystery Stories

THE
CRISSCROSS
SHADOW

BY

FRANKLIN W. DIXON

NEW YORK
GROSSET & DUNLAP
Publishers

CONTENTS

CONTENTS

THE CRISSCROSS SHADOW

CHAPTER I

A Strange Sale

"I WANT to speak to my nephews Frank and Joe Hardy at once," said an excited voice on the telephone. "It's urgent."

"Yes, Miss Hardy," replied the manager of Bayport High's football team. "They're out on the field. I'll get 'em."

Meanwhile, on the thirty-yard line Coach Devlin was saying, "Okay, team, let's run through our new defensive play once more."

The eleven lined up, the regulars on defense, the scrubs facing them.

"86X," barked Frank Hardy, captain and quarterback, as the opposing center moved over the pigskin.

The ball was snapped. At the same instant, stocky Chet Morton, the regulars' stalwart center, pulled out of the line to cover the left flank. The scrubs' halfback darted up and over the line of scrimmage.

"Tackle him, Chet, tackle him!" shouted Frank.

Chet plowed into the second-string ball carrier and brought him to the ground for no gain.

"Good going, boys," said Coach Devlin. "I think you've got that defensive play down pretty well. Once around the field and then into the showers," he said, dismissing them.

Frank and his brother Joe, a year younger, jogged along together. Lithe, blond-haired Joe, who played left halfback, was puffing.

"Coach really had us working on that 86X, didn't he?"

"I'll say he did," tall, dark-haired Frank replied. "But it's going to come in mighty handy when we play Hopkinsville—"

"Frank! Joe!" the manager called out. "Telephone call for you. Better hurry. Your aunt seems very excited!"

The brothers looked at each other wonderingly. Sons of Fenton Hardy, the famous detective, they were accomplished sleuths themselves in spite of their youth. They had often received urgent calls but never in a locker room!

Joe hurried to the phone. "Hello," he said anxiously.

"Joe, is that you?" asked a crisp feminine voice. "This is Aunt Gertrude."

"What's up?"

Aunt Gertrude, who was staying at the Hardy

home, was the boys' favorite relative. Though she did not hesitate on occasion to reprimand her nephews, they had great respect for her insight into human nature.

"There's a strange salesman in the house," Aunt Gertrude reported. "He's trying to sell your mother some leather goods, but I don't like his looks. I'm sure he's a swindler. I've seen his picture somewhere in the papers."

Joe whistled softly. "We'll come right home, Auntie," he promised.

The boys did not wait to shower or change their clothes, but hurried to their convertible.

Since their father was away on a secret mission to the West Coast—so secret that he had not even told the boys about it—Frank and Joe felt a protective responsibility toward the two women at home.

As he maneuvered the sleek car through Bayport's busy streets, Frank wore a puzzled frown.

"I don't like this at all, Joe," he said.

"Let's have a look-see through the window before we go in," Joe suggested. "You know what Dad says. A little undercover sleuthing in advance is better than barging in head on."

"Good idea."

When they reached the tree-lined neighborhood where the Hardy home was located, Frank proceeded cautiously.

"We'll park here," he said, quietly turning off the

motor and gliding to the curb about three hundred feet from the house.

The boys went up a neighbor's driveway, crossed the back yard, and approached their own house from the rear.

"How about looking in the side living-room window?" Frank whispered. Joe nodded.

Tiptoeing up the driveway, the boys flattened themselves against the side of the house below the window. Cautiously they lifted their heads until their eyes were on a level with the sill. A strange man, his back to them, was there alone.

Suddenly Joe gave a start and said, "He just took something off Mother's desk!"

"What is it?" Frank asked. "I can't make it out— oh, yes—it's Dad's key case!"

As the youthful detectives watched, the man, unaware that he was being observed, opened the case and quickly slipped a key off one of the rings.

The boys waited to see no more. Dashing around the house, they unlocked the door and ran into the hall.

"Why, hello, boys," a pleasant feminine voice said. Mrs. Hardy was descending the stairway. "What brings you home so early from practice—and in your football uniforms?"

"Hello, Mother!" they answered together, as they followed her into the living room, then Joe burst out:

"This man is what brings us home."

"I don't understand," she replied, as the stranger stared at them with an air of surprise.

"Why did you pick up my father's key case and take a key from it?" Frank asked accusingly.

"What do you mean?" the stranger flared.

"Frank! Joe!" their mother exclaimed, taken aback by her sons' actions. "You'd better apologize to Mr. Breck. I have just purchased a new key case from him for your father."

"And I was merely transferring the old ones to the new case while your mother went for her pocket-book," Mr. Breck said triumphantly.

Embarrassed, the boys looked at the two cases. There were three keys in the new one.

"Here is a letter of introduction Mr. Breck brought from Mrs. Wilson," their mother quickly explained as she handed them a folded sheet of paper.

Her sons scanned the typewritten letter, which told what a reliable man Mr. Breck was and how reasonably he was selling fine handmade leather articles. At the bottom of the page was a signature which the boys recognized as that of an old friend of their mother and father.

As they looked up, Mr. Breck gazed straight at the boys. A taunting smile outlined the lips of the dark, burly man who looked to be about thirty-five years old.

"No reason to get excited," he said smoothly. "I've just been showing your mother some beautiful hand-tooled leather goods. She's bought a wallet, a hand-bag—"

Breck stopped speaking and looked flustered when he saw Miss Hardy in the doorway. Tall, stern Aunt Gertrude stood there glaring in unfriendly fashion. But the salesman recovered himself quickly.

"Oh, another customer," he said.

"Indeed not," stated the boys' aunt firmly. "Laura," she addressed her sister-in-law, "are you sure this man is—?"

"Say, what is this, a courtroom?" Breck cried out angrily.

"Oh, please," Mrs. Hardy begged, greatly distressed.

Meanwhile, Joe had been silently counting the keys. He did this twice to make certain how many were there. He knew the exact number there should be because Mr. Hardy, shortly before he left, had given the keys to his wife in Joe's presence. The boy's sleuthing instinct had prompted him to count them at that time. Now one key was missing!

"Mr. Breck," he demanded, his eyes flashing, "what did you do with a thin, brass key that was in this old case?"

"Why . . . why . . ." the stranger stammered, hunting for words. "How dare you accuse me of stealing a key?"

"I'm accusing you, all right," Joe went on. "There's a key missing—a special one. Hand it over!"

"I haven't got one of the keys, you young whipper-snapper," the man replied indignantly. "Your father probably took it with him. You have a nerve accusing me of being a thief. I'm an honest salesman." Breck's voice grew rough.

"Please!" Mrs. Hardy interrupted. "Mr. Hardy, no doubt, removed the key himself."

"I'm not going to stay here and be insulted any longer," Breck exclaimed, his dark face red with anger.

He moved to his small suitcase, tossed his samples inside, and snapped it shut.

"I'm getting out of this house," he said hotly. "Why, I've never been treated so rudely in my life. I've had enough of your insinuations."

Joe made a move to detain the salesman. But his mother forbade it.

"Let him go, Joe," she advised. "No key is worth such a scene."

"But, Mother, it's the one to the file in Dad's study—"

"We still don't know that your father didn't take it."

The boys were reluctant to let the man go, but their mother's word was law. Breck then stalked out, slamming the front door behind him.

Mrs. Hardy, still looking distressed, commented: "I know you don't trust the man, Frank and Joe. But I did hate to have a scene, especially since there was no proof against him."

"Sure, I understand," Frank answered. "Though the way he acted was mighty suspicious."

"I'll say," Joe agreed. "He'd better not show his face around here again."

The boys went upstairs, removed their football gear, and showered.

Five minutes later, while they were dressing, they heard Aunt Gertrude cry out. As the boys were speculating about what had happened, she knocked on their door.

"Hurry up! Go find that man Breck. He's stolen your father's picture!"

Pulling on sweaters, they opened the door, and followed her downstairs. Mrs. Hardy was staring at the top of the baby grand piano where her husband's photograph had stood for nearly a year.

"I guess you were right after all about that salesman," she said. "He's taken Dad's picture. But why?"

"We'll find out!" Frank cried.

Together the boys raced from the house and down the street to their car. They had little hope of locating Breck, but to their relief Joe spotted him in the center of town walking hurriedly along the sidewalk.

The convertible pulled up even with him. As it came to a stop, he glanced at the boys, then started to run.

Leaping from the car, the boys gave chase. But Breck had a head start. He turned the corner. When the Hardys reached it, the man was not in sight!

CHAPTER II

A Clever Alibi

"WHERE'D Breck go?" Joe cried, dismayed that their quarry had eluded them.

He and Frank glanced at both sides of the deserted street, seeing nothing but a few parked cars.

Suddenly Joe cried out. "Look, between those two parked cars. Isn't that a suitcase? And a man? Come on, Frank."

The boys dashed across the street. Joe approached the space between the cars from the sidewalk, Frank from the street.

"There he is! Grab him, Joe!" Frank exclaimed as Breck, aware that he had been sighted, tried to make a getaway.

Joe, executing a perfect tackle, stopped the man dead in his tracks. Grunting and panting, Breck tried to shake him off, but Frank, coming up from behind, pinned the husky salesman's shoulders to the ground, while his brother clung grimly to his legs.

"Let me up! Get off!" Breck cried, struggling to rise.

"Not until we've searched you," replied Frank, holding him even more tightly.

Just then Joe caught sight of a policeman sauntering along on the other side of the street.

"Hey, Casey!" he shouted to the officer, whom they had known for years. "We can use some help!"

Seeing the boys and their struggling captive, Casey broke into a run.

"What's up, fellows?" he cried as he reached them.

Frank and Joe released their grip on Breck, who now made no effort to break away.

This man stole a picture of my father and the key to his file cabinet," Frank replied, pointing to Breck who glowered at the boys.

"Yes, we want him searched," Joe chimed in.

"All right," the officer's voice was stern. "Come along to headquarters, mister."

"Our car's around the corner," Frank said.

Breck started to object, but the policeman silenced him with a gesture.

"I never question Frank and Joe's judgment," he stated as they walked to the boys' convertible. "I guess you don't know that they're sons of the famous detective Fenton Hardy. And they're right smart detectives themselves. Solved lots of cases, like *The Tower Treasure*. And not long ago they went out west and tangled with some bad characters in *The Secret of Wildcat Swamp*."

Arriving at police headquarters, the group was met by Chief Ezra Collig, grizzled veteran of many a battle with Bayport's criminal elements. He and the Hardys had often worked together in rounding up underworld characters.

"Well, now, who's this man, boys?" the chief asked briskly. "What's he been up to?"

The brothers quickly explained the mysterious activities of Breck.

"We can prove it, too!" exclaimed Joe, referring to the thefts of the picture and key. "All you've got to do is search him."

"No, you don't," Breck protested. "I insist upon calling my lawyer. You've got to permit that. I know my rights," he added threateningly.

"Okay," the officer agreed. "Who's your lawyer?"

"Miles Kamp," Breck replied quickly.

"Miles Kamp, eh? I've never heard of him. Must be a stranger to Bayport."

Frank and Joe looked at Breck suspiciously as the man dialed the phone on the chief's desk. After a few guarded words to Kamp, he hung up, a look of satisfaction on his face.

Ten minutes later Miles Kamp strode into the chief's office. He was a short, heavy-jowled man with a wide thin-lipped mouth that suggested a nasty streak in his character. He peered at them near-sightedly through thick-lensed glasses.

Frank turned to Joe. "I don't like his looks, do

you?" he whispered to his brother as the salesman shook hands with the lawyer.

"No," the younger Hardy replied. "He looks even more suspicious than Breck."

"Now, now what's going on here?" he said in an annoyed voice. "Why are you holding my client? I demand to know the meaning of this."

The nearsighted little lawyer flailed his arms wildly.

"Calm down, Mr. Kamp," Chief Collig said to him sternly. "Mr. Breck is accused of stealing a key and a photograph belonging to Fenton Hardy, the detective. These are his sons, and they want this man searched."

"Searched? Why, certainly, my client will gladly agree to this. He has nothing to hide," Kamp replied pompously. "Mr. Breck," he said, turning to the leather goods salesman whose face wore a smug look, "I advise you to let the police search you. We know you have nothing to fear."

At Chief Collig's order the policeman went to work. He turned Breck's pockets inside out and made him remove his shoes. Then he looked through the man's suitcase.

"Nothing suspicious here, boys," he reported.

Frank's eyes were intent on a bulge under the man's shirt. "What are you hiding there?" he asked.

The policeman investigated and found a framed photograph of Fenton Hardy.

"What was the idea of taking that?" Joe said accusingly.

Breck's face began to redden. "Well . . . well, you see . . ." the salesman stammered in embarrassment. "You're right. I *did* take your father's picture, and I apologize," he confessed sheepishly. "But I can explain."

"You'd better have a good reason," the chief interrupted.

"You see, I've always been a great admirer of Fenton Hardy," Breck went on rapidly, "and I've followed his exploits for years. So today, when I saw his picture on the piano, I couldn't resist picking it up as a souvenir."

"Well, that puts things in a somewhat different light," said Chief Collig slowly, his suspicions allayed.

"I knew you'd understand," Breck continued hastily. "And I hope the boys do. I'd like to keep the photo. It would mean a lot to me." There was a note of sincerity in his voice.

"I don't know," Joe replied slowly, looking at his brother questioningly.

"Please let me have it," Breck pleaded. "I'll give you back the frame. All I want is the photograph of Mr. Hardy."

"Hmmph—" Chief Collig began, as all looked to him for advice. "The picture isn't autographed, is it?" he asked, scanning the photograph.

"No. Dad didn't autograph this one," Joe replied quickly.

"Well," the officer continued soberly, "as long as it's not signed, and since Fenton Hardy's picture has appeared so frequently in newspapers anyway, I don't see what harm there'd be if this man keeps it. Since Mr. Breck didn't take the key, we have no special charge to hold him. But it's up to you boys to decide, of course," he concluded.

Breck turned to Frank and Joe, a hopeful expression on his face. There were several moments of silence, during which Miles Kamp pulled out a handkerchief and made a great show of polishing his glasses. All eyes turned on the Hardys.

The boys looked at each other again. Years of working closely together had given each one the uncanny ability to know at a glance what the other was thinking.

Frank spoke. "I guess it's all right for him to keep the picture, as long as he's such a great admirer of Dad's."

"All right. He can have it," Joe agreed.

"Thank you, thank you. I can't tell you how happy this makes me. It's very generous of you," said Breck effusively.

He moved impulsively to grasp the hands of the Hardy boys to show his gratitude. Frank and Joe acknowledged his thanks coolly, their dislike of the man by no means lessened.

"Well, Chief Collig," interrupted Kamp in his pompous voice, "are you satisfied that my client has done nothing wrong? If so, I suggest you release him immediately."

"All right, you can go," the officer replied. Then he added sternly, eying the salesman with disfavor. "But I'm warning you, Breck, in the future you'd better not be helping yourself to pictures in people's houses."

"Thank you, Chief Collig," said Kamp unctuously. "We appreciate your co-operation. Good day to you," he addressed the boys.

With a bow he strutted from the room, Breck at his heels.

"Breck won this round," remarked Frank. "But I still don't put any stock in his explanations."

"I know what you mean," agreed Collig. "We don't have a thing to hold him on, though."

A little while later, driving home in the convertible, Joe turned to Frank.

"Did you notice the back of Breck's hand as he was packing his suitcase?" he asked his brother.

"Yes," Frank replied. "He had a strange-looking scar on the back of it in the shape of a W. You couldn't miss it."

"If he were a thief, it sure would be easy to spot him," Joe replied. "By the way, remember what Aunt Gertrude said about having seen his picture somewhere identifying him as a criminal?"

"That's right. We'll have to check with her on that."

Reaching home, the boys hurried up the steps. They knew supper would be ready and they were looking forward to a delicious steak dinner.

"Hope Aunt Gertrude has apple pie to go with it." Joe grinned, anticipating the tasty meal that had been promised.

"I could eat at least two helpings," declared Frank as they entered the hall.

There they found Aunt Gertrude, greatly agitated. She was waiting for them.

"Joe! Frank!" cried the tall, graying lady. "I was right about that so-called leather salesman all the time!"

"You mean about having seen his picture somewhere?" Frank asked.

"No, not that. But I just called Mrs. Wilson, the one whose name was on the reference Breck showed us."

"Yes?"

"Just as I suspected," their aunt continued triumphantly. "Mrs. Wilson said that she never saw the man in her life. That reference was forged!"

CHAPTER III

A Dangerous Visit

"WHAT!" Frank cried. "Mrs. Wilson never heard of Breck?"

Aunt Gertrude shook her head.

"Then he forged the signature," Joe added. "Well, we sure were taken in. That guy probably had the key all the time—in his mouth maybe."

"And slipped it to Kamp. Joe, how could we be so dumb?"

"Anyway, we can try to find him. I want to question him further."

"Not until we get a new lock for Dad's file," Frank said emphatically. "After going to all that trouble to get the key, Breck might try to use it!"

"Right you are!"

The boys excused themselves and hurried to a trusted locksmith with whom their father dealt. He supplied them with a new lock and instructed them how to install it.

18

After Frank and Joe had arrived home and had just replaced the old lock, a voice behind them said:

"Neat job, fellows!"

The boys whirled. "Sam Radley!" they exclaimed, and hurried across the room to greet their visitor.

"Hello," Sam replied cheerily, shaking hands with them.

Sam Radley was Fenton Hardy's able assistant, and the boys knew him well because he had helped them solve many a tough problem. They had not seen him in several weeks and knew that he had been on a top-secret assignment with their father. They hoped he had news of Mr. Hardy.

"You'll stay to supper, Sam?" Mrs. Hardy invited, coming into the room. "That'll give us a chance to hear about your case."

"Thank you. I'd like to."

"How's Dad?" Joe asked after they sat down. "You've been working with him, haven't you?"

Sam smiled. "Yes, I have. Your father's fine."

"What's the case about?" Frank put in. "Or can't you tell us?"

"Just a little," the detective replied, choosing his words carefully. "Your dad and I are working for the government. There have been several cases of sabotage in important industries throughout the country.

"It looks as though these cases are part of some master plan. We think the same gang is involved in all of them, but so far we haven't been able to find any clues that point to the guilty persons. That's about all I can tell you," Sam concluded.

Frank gave a long, low whistle. "Sounds like an important—and dangerous—case."

"We're working on a mystery of our own," interposed Joe.

Briefly, the boys recounted the events of the past few hours, ending with Aunt Gertrude's report of the forged letter of reference.

"That man Breck!" their aunt expostulated. "I just know I've seen his picture in connection with something dishonest. Land sakes, I've been around detectives long enough to know a suspicious character when I see one!" she exclaimed.

"You're better at it than I am," Mrs. Hardy remarked ruefully. "But then, you're Fenton's sister."

"And just the person to help us find Breck," Frank said. "We'll go to police headquarters in the morning and look at their rogues' gallery."

Directly after breakfast the next day the boys drove her downtown. She marched purposefully into headquarters, followed by her nephews. It was obvious that Aunt Gertrude meant to find out where she had seen the thief's picture. The boys knew that it was wise to keep in the background when she was in that mood.

"Good morning, Chief," she greeted Collig, as the trio was ushered into his office.

"Aunt Gertrude wants to look at your rogues' gallery file to see if she can identify Breck," Frank informed the officer.

"Well, well, so they're making a detective out of you, too," he joked, showing Aunt Gertrude several thin albums of pictures which lay on a table.

Miss Hardy leafed through the pages slowly. Suddenly she gave a start. "That looks as if it might be Breck," she said excitedly.

"It might be," replied Joe, peering over her shoulder, "except that it's 'Jerry the Character' Slocomb, and he's in the federal penitentiary this minute for counterfeiting."

"Gracious sakes," responded Aunt Gertrude. "Well, what about him?" she asked, pointing to another photograph. "He certainly looks like Breck."

"Yes, he does," admitted Frank, "but that man was picked up a couple of days ago on the West Coast for forgery. That's 'Fancy Fingers' Finley."

Collig laughed. "Miss Hardy, you got to do better than that."

"I'll find him yet," Aunt Gertrude said with determination.

"Maybe if you come along with us to find him—" Joe suggested half-jokingly.

"And don't think I wouldn't capture him if I did!" she retorted. "Just the same, good detectives can stay right at home and solve certain mysteries. They don't have to gallivant all over the countryside."

"Armchair detectives, eh?" Frank laughed. "Well, I don't want to be that kind. I'll take action. Want to come with us? We have a school holiday."

"No, I'm staying right here. And you are, too, until I finish. I'll prove my point yet."

For the next hour she pored over the pictures. Every once in a while she would pause at one which resembled Breck. Finally she closed the last album with a sigh of disappointment.

"He's just not here," Aunt Gertrude said dejectedly. "But I know I've seen his picture somewhere," she vowed.

"Maybe he was in disguise, Aunt Gertrude," Joe suggested. He was disappointed, too, that she had not been able to put her finger on a photograph of the mysterious man, and neither he nor Frank could find him.

After telling Collig of the man's forgery, Frank asked for Breck's address.

"We'd better work quickly before Breck decides to leave town!" Frank said.

The officer consulted his files for a moment. "Breck's registered at the Excelsior Hotel, boys," he informed them, mentioning the name of a third-rate hotel in the water-front section of Bayport.

After dropping off Aunt Gertrude who wanted to do some shopping, the boys drove to the Excelsior.

"Have you a man named Wylie Breck staying here?" Frank asked the clerk.

The man consulted the register. "We did," he replied after a moment, "but he checked out."

The boys looked at each other in disappointment. "I know," said Frank. "Let's phone his lawyer Miles Kamp. Maybe he can tell us where Breck is."

The boys hurried to a telephone booth. After a few moments, Kamp answered.

"Yes, this is Miles Kamp," came the familiar pompous voice. "May I be of service to you?" he inquired.

Frank asked where he could find Breck.

"I'm dreadfully sorry, my boy, but I can't help you at all. I haven't the vaguest idea where Breck went."

As Frank hung up, he wondered if this were the truth. He reported to Joe.

"No help from that source," he commented in disgust.

"He knows very well where Breck is," Joe declared.

As the brothers passed the desk again, the clerk beckoned to them. They hurried over.

"Aren't you Frank and Joe Hardy?" he asked.

The boys admitted that they were.

"I thought so," the clerk continued in a low tone. "I recognized you from your newspaper pictures. I didn't care much for that guy Breck. If you're tracking him down, I'll let you look through his room for any possible clues. Follow me."

"Thanks," Frank said.

A minute later the clerk let them into the vacant room, then started back downstairs.

The boys searched thoroughly, looking into drawers, the wastebasket, even under the mattress, but could not find a clue to the mysterious leather goods salesman.

"Looks as if we're stuck," Joe said dejectedly to his brother as they came out of the room.

"Maybe not. There's a chambermaid. Let's see if she knows anything about Breck," Frank suggested. He had caught sight of a woman coming down the corridor carrying a pile of linen.

The boys approached the chambermaid and Frank explained that they were looking for some trace of Breck.

"Breck, Breck," repeated the woman slowly. "Seems like I recall the feller. Hard-looking chap. Shooed me out of the room once. Acted very strange like."

Suddenly her face lit up. "I do remember something!" she exclaimed. "A bit of brown wrapping paper."

Going to a closet, she began to dig through a pile of trash. Presently the chambermaid gave a triumphant cry.

"Here it is!" she called. "I emptied this out of Breck's room."

The boys scanned the paper hurriedly.

"I can make out a name, Philip York," Frank exclaimed. "But the address is blurred!"

"Philip York," his brother repeated. "I wonder if he could be a friend of Breck's."

Taking the paper to a window, Frank held it to let the light strike it obliquely. In this way, he had often deciphered smeared or smudged writing.

"Here's a return address! It says," Frank went on, reading haltingly, "twenty-four Dock Street, South . . . South . . . South*port*," he concluded triumphantly.

The address was that of a town several miles from Bayport on Eagle Bay, where the boys had often gone cruising.

"Come on, Frank!" Joe urged excitedly. "Let's go to Southport and call on this Philip York!"

They thanked the maid for her help and hurried from the hotel. A few minutes later the two young detectives were on their way to Southport.

Within half an hour Frank was guiding their convertible through the crowded streets of the grimy water-front section of Southport. Reaching Dock Street, Joe began to look at the house numbers.

"There it is!" he exclaimed. "Pull up, Frank."

Twenty-four Dock Street was a ramshackle tenement. As the boys walked through the open front door, a stocky man dressed in dirty work clothes brushed rudely by them into the hallway.

"Frank," Joe whispered, "he might be York."

With a bound, the boys followed the man up the rickety stairs.

"Say, mister," Joe called out, "we want to ask you some questions."

The man turned around and faced them. "Who do you think you're following?" he asked angrily.

"We want some information," Frank said boldly.

"So you want info, do ya?" the man replied. "Well, who are you and what's your business here? G'wan. Get out of here before I throw you out." He raised his arm in a threatening motion.

Undaunted, the boys held their ground.

"You'll throw nobody out," said Frank in a quiet but determined voice. "Do you know a Wylie Breck?"

"No."

"Are you Philip York?"

The man surveyed the boys standing shoulder to shoulder. "No, I'm not," he answered. "What's the racket?"

Frank shrugged. "We heard they lived here. Thought we'd look 'em up."

"Oh, that's different. Well, I never heard of Wylie Breck, but there's a Philip York on the first floor," the stranger went on, somewhat calmed down.

The man pointed down the stairs. "He lives in that apartment. But I advise you kids to scram. You don't belong here. You'll get into trouble." The man went up the stairs without explaining further.

Frank and Joe, undaunted by the warning, descended the stairs. The hallway was dark and had a musty odor. They rapped on the door of York's apartment.

After a few moments' wait they heard footsteps approaching the door.

"Get set, Frank, in case it's Breck and he slams the door in our faces," Joe whispered.

As the door was flung open the boys tensed themselves.

"What do you want?" An unshaven man, wearing a royal-blue sweater, challenged them. He was not Breck.

"We're looking for Wylie Breck and Philip York," Frank replied quickly, edging closer to the door.

"Breck? York?" the man rasped in a foggy voice. "Never heard of 'em. What business you got in this place, anyway?" he asked.

"We want to talk to them, that's all," Frank replied. "Maybe you've seen Breck around."

Frank described Breck, adding that he carried a suitcase full of leather goods.

"Never saw him," the man said.

Suddenly he raised his eyes and looked beyond the boys. Alert to danger, the boys turned.

As the door slammed behind them, they saw two dark shapes coming swiftly toward them.

"Look out!" Joe cried.

CHAPTER IV

The Telltale Moccasin

THE BROTHERS were only half turned to meet the attack when the two men crashed into them, chest high. Joe was knocked out, Frank stunned.

The older boy instinctively lashed out at the men with both fists. One of the attackers sank to his knees after Frank connected with an uppercut to the jaw, but the other thug, coming from behind, got a strangle hold on the boy which rendered him helpless.

The boys' assailants dragged them down the hallway, pushed them into a closet, and locked the door.

"Leave the key in," a voice ordered.

It was several seconds before Joe regained his senses and remembered what had happened.

"Who could those guys have been?" Frank was saying as he rammed his body against the door to open it.

"Beats me. Let's try pounding first," Joe advised. "We don't want to pay for a broken door."

They thumped on the panel and waited. Hearing no one, they began yelling:

"Help! Help!"

Presently they heard heavy footsteps coming down the hall. Was he friend or foe?

"I'm going to tackle him whoever he is," Joe said.

Before Frank could warn against it, the door opened and Joe charged the man outside. The two of them rolled on the floor in a heap.

"I've got him, Frank!" he cried.

"Hey, lay off, fellows!" a familiar voice shouted.

"Chet Morton!" Frank exclaimed, recognizing their friend and helping him to his feet.

"Chet, how the dickens did you get here?" Joe demanded. "Gee, I'm sorry. I thought you might be one of the thugs who threw us in the closet."

"Hm," said Chet as he dusted himself off. "I thought you would get in trouble, so I followed you from Bayport. My jalopy can't tear like yours. I nearly lost you, but a kid on the corner told me where you went."

"Why'd you follow us?" Frank asked.

"Did you forget that we play Hopkinsville on Saturday? The team wants you to be in good shape for it."

"Good thing you came, Chet," Joe replied. "Sorry I was rough with you."

"That's okay," Chet said lightly. "Centers ought to be ready for surprise tackles."

"Let's talk again to that fellow in the blue sweater," Frank proposed. "Maybe he knows who hit us. I wonder if they live in this tenement house."

The trio hurried down the corridor, and Joe rapped on the door. No one answered. He pounded.

"Mighty mysterious," Frank commented. "That fellow knew we were in trouble. If he isn't in league with them, why didn't he help us out?"

"He must be a friend of Breck's," Joe replied. "And that's why he didn't tell us that he was Philip York."

No one came to open the door. Either the man had gone out or for reasons of his own would not answer.

"Let's report this whole business to the Southport police," said Frank. "There's nothing more we can do here."

"Now you're talking," agreed Chet. "This is a good place to stay away from."

After they had made a full statement at headquarters, and asked the sergeant to report any developments to Chief Collig, the boys drove back to Bayport in their own cars.

Frank and Joe were puzzled by the day's events, but their determination to find Breck was stronger than ever.

Arriving home, they were greeted by their mother.

"Come on, boys," she said. "Hurry and wash. There's a good supper waiting for you."

After supper, which included a second helping of their mother's chocolate walnut cake, Frank said:

"Joe, I have an idea. Why don't we try tracking down the manufacturer of that key case Mother bought from Breck? In that way, perhaps we'll be able to find out who Breck really is."

"Smart brother. Let's start now."

The boys went into their father's study, where Mrs. Hardy had put the new key case. Joe turned it over carefully in his hand. There was no name on it.

"But here's something inside," he announced.

Imprinted on the leather, in a corner of the case, was an odd mark:

The boys gave a sigh of satisfaction.

"Now we've got something definite to go on," Frank said, smiling. "Tomorrow we'll show it to a leather goods dealer and ask him what manufacturer uses this mark."

After football practice the next afternoon, they hurried straight to the shop of their white-haired friend Mr. Nobbly. Frank drew the key case from his pocket.

"We'd like to find out who made this," he explained. "Here's the imprint. Can you tell us who uses this trade-mark?"

Mr. Nobbly examined the mark closely. He shook his head slowly.

"Sorry, boys," the shopkeeper answered. "I never heard of nor saw that mark in all my thirty-five years in this business."

"Then it's probably some private maker's?" Frank asked.

"No doubt. It's fine, hand-tooled work. But it would be like hunting for a penny in the mud of Barmet Bay to find him."

Frank looked at Joe in disappointment. Another clue gone up in smoke!

"Come on," Joe said. "We'll keep checking on this."

They thanked Mr. Nobbly and left the store. For the next few days the Hardys called at every possible place in their quest for a clue to the maker of the key case with the strange R imprint.

They went to all the leather goods shops in Bayport and examined key cases, wallets, handbags, and luggage. They even checked with shoe stores. But to no avail. No one in Bayport had ever seen such a mark.

Finally, the boys had to postpone continuing their search for a lead on Breck and settle down to hard football practice. Saturday came with the big game against Hopkinsville.

Frank was gloomy as the team donned their uniforms in the locker room.

"I guess it's no use trying to trace that symbol," he said dejectedly to Joe, pulling on his jersey.

"Looks like you're right," his brother replied. "Well, let's forget about it for a while. We have a game to play, and you know what a whale of a team Hopkinsville has this year."

As the boys trotted along the corridor of the field house, Frank spied a moccasin lying on the cement floor. Ordinarily he would not have done any more than kick it out of the way. But being interested now in everything made of leather he bent down and picked it up.

"Joe, look!" he exulted. "The mark! The telltale mark!"

"Sure enough," Joe cried. "I wonder who dropped this."

He queried the members of his team as they came from the field house. None owned the moccasin.

"Must be someone from Hopkinsville," Frank mused. "We'll find out later."

He took it along and laid it on the bench. The warm-up period was over and they were waiting for the whistle when one of the Hopkinsville players ran by. He noticed Frank holding the moccasin.

"Say, what are you fellows doing with that?" he asked. "It belongs to one of our ends—George Parks."

"Where is he?" inquired Joe. "We want to ask him about this moccasin."

The Hopkinsville player pointed. "He's the tall guy there."

At that moment the referee blew his whistle, signaling that the game was to begin.

The biggest crowd in years had gathered to watch the contest. Hopkinsville won the toss and elected to defend the north goal with the wind at their backs. Frank and Joe waited tensely in their positions as the Hopkinsville booter carefully placed the ball for the kickoff.

"Here it comes!" Frank cried. "Joe, it's headed right for you!"

Joe caught the end-over-end kickoff on the ten-yard line. Twisting and dodging, he carried the ball to mid-field. The Bayport stands cheered loudly.

Frank gained a couple of yards on the next play on a smash through tackle. Then, on the following play, Joe faded back and tossed a short pass to left end, played by Tony Prito. The dark-haired, wiry youth, a close friend of the Hardys, took the ball for a first down on the Hopkinsville thirty-five.

A couple of line bucks by Biff Hooper, another of their special friends, gained a few yards, and finally on the fourth down Joe faded back for a long pass.

Frank shot down the field like a streak of lightning, the ball sailing straight toward him. But just as he was reaching for it, a Hopkinsville player batted it down, and the opponents took over.

Frank moved along behind his linemen, grunting words of confidence to each in turn. "Let's get in there now! Let's hold 'em!"

The Hopkinsville quarterback wheeled about into a long sweeping fake motion to the left. Their fast right halfback, in the fullback slot, took a soft pass from center, let his interference form, and behind his two low-running blockers, sped out toward the right side, ready to cut in when he could.

He found his hole, shot through it, and raced out into the open!

Joe came up from his safety position, moving diagonally to force the ball carrier to the side line. He drove him off side with a beautiful tackle on the Bayport nine-yard line.

But it was first down and goal to go!

In three plays Hopkinsville was on the Bayport four!

"This is the big one," Frank thought. "We've got to hold. This is the time to call the secret defensive play we've been practicing all week."

As the teams lined up for fourth down, Frank called out crisply:

"86X!"

Both Bayport tackles, instead of making the usual defensive charge, remained fixed in their positions and let the offensive linemen come to them. Through the tiny space created by this forward motion, Chet and Frank knifed into the enemy backfield and made havoc of the play, Chet making the tackle and stopping Newman, the Hopkinsville ace, in his tracks. The secret play had worked! The threat was halted! The remainder of the period was chiefly a punting duel between Frank and Newman. Each would run two ground plays and then punt. After several such exchanges, it became clear that Frank was getting more yardage with his high booming kicks that spiraled deep into enemy territory every time.

The Hopkinsville coach changed his strategy. He called a fresh end off the bench, briefed him with an arm around his thick shoulders, and sent him into the game. The team seemed to get a new life as he came trotting on. This meant their favorite pass play!

Joe, just before he dropped back to his safety zone, got a quick glimpse of the replacement. He recognized him as George Parks!

"Now I'll be able to find out about the moccasin," Joe thought, but his excitement was lost in the barking of signals by the Hopkinsville quarterback.

Parks drifted down field, got by Chet, and was lengthening his stride to take a long pass over his right shoulder, when Joe came racing across and knocked the ball right off his finger tips.

Joe ran back a few steps to pick up the ball. Tossing it to the referee, he turned quickly to talk to George Parks about the moccasin. But Parks had left the game and was almost off the field! He had been sent in for one play and that was all.

The first half ended in a scoreless tie. Each team went directly to its locker room.

As the Hardys came running side by side onto the field for the second half, Frank whispered to Joe, "We'll speak to Parks right after the game. That moccasin is a vital clue."

CHAPTER V

Indian Surprise

AFTER the half-time interval Joe fastened his head-gear a little more securely, took a reassuring look at George Parks on the Hopkinsville bench, and signaled for the kickoff.

The whole period was a seesaw affair, with each team getting breaks and losing them. Once a fumble by Bayport deep in its own territory gave the enemy a chance to score, but a brilliant interception by Frank smothered that threat.

The period ended with the teams still deadlocked in a 0–0 tie. And now Hopkinsville, as they lined up at the other end of the field, had the strong wind at their backs!

"They'll throw a hundred passes," Frank muttered to Chet just before play began. But for some reason they didn't. They tried a series of line smashes and were finally stopped. The punting duel resumed, with Newman getting the advantage.

Time was beginning to run out. Then, with two short pass completions, and a thirty-yard run by Frank, Bayport moved down to the Hopkinsville twenty. With only a minute and a half to play, Chet smashed off his left tackle for a gain of four yards, to the sixteen-yard line, but he was hit hard. He fumbled! Hopkinsville recovered!

One minute remained. Without calling a huddle, and taking a direct pass from center, Newman, leaping straight up, threw a floating pass straight down the alley for twenty yards. First and ten!

"Now they'll be throwing," Frank said to himself.

The enemy ends crossed and the ball was thrown to the same spot as before. An end gathered it in and was off. He was hit on the Bayport forty.

Newman was fading again. Another pass. The same kind. Another ten-yard gain. First and ten for Hopkinsville on the Bayport twenty!

The stands were in a frenzy. There was no stopping Newman. He was hitting his man on every pitch.

With seconds to go, the Hopkinsville team suddenly fanned out in a widespread formation. Bayport shifted with them. Newman called his signals. Suddenly Joe noticed that Chet had not shifted. He was standing with a dazed look on his face. Then it dawned on Joe!

Each pass had been made into Chet's zone. He must have been hurt on that line smash. No doubt Newman would be throwing in there again!

The ball was snapped to Newman. He began to fade way back. He threw a long, lazy pass that soared over Chet's head toward the Bayport goal line.

The timekeeper's gun sounded as the ball was in flight. As soon as the ball was dead now, the game would be officially over!

Joe, who had anticipated the play, was at the goal line, a step ahead of the Bayport pass receiver. He leaped up, wrenched the ball out of the grasp of his opponent, whirled, and scooted across the field, just outside of his own goal line. All around him Hopkinsville men were being knocked down with clean, jarring blocks. Joe was away!

At the fifty-yard line, he reversed his field. Frank threw a vicious block at the fastest enemy tackler, and Joe sprinted into the clear, with the wild uproar of the Bayport stands in his ears, straight down the side line to the Hopkinsville goal.

The score was Bayport 6, Hopkinsville 0! Pandemonium reigned!

As Frank sent the ball straight through the crossbars, the gun sounded the end of the game.

Bayport had won 7-0 on Joe Hardy's one-hundred-yard dash for a touchdown! Frank hugged his brother, delirious with joy.

"What a run! There's never been a touchdown run that long in the history of Bayport High!"

"Yeah, Hardy boys!" the Bayport fans shouted as they poured out on the field. "Up with 'em!"

With cheers and singing, they were borne off the field on the shoulders of their teammates. When at last they were set down, more fans crowded around to pommel the boys and shake their hands.

"Joe! Joe!" Frank shouted over the tumult. "We must see George Parks before he gets away."

But the boys were trapped by their admirers, as the Hopkinsville team dejectedly disappeared from the field. Fifteen minutes went by.

"We'll have to break loose," Joe finally called to Frank.

"Yes," his brother agreed, "come on. Let's go!"

Shouldering their way through the cheering crowd, the boys broke into a run for the field house.

"Where's the Hopkinsville team?" Joe asked the janitor breathlessly, as they reached the visitors' locker room.

"Why, I reckon they're getting ready to go home in their school bus," the old fellow replied.

Racing to the parking lot, the boys saw the Hopkinsville bus pulling out.

"Hey, wait a minute!" Joe cried.

The boys gave chase, but it was too late. In a cloud of dust, the bus disappeared down the road, leaving the young detectives panting in the roadway.

As they trudged back toward the field house, Joe said, "I wonder what Parks did about his moccasin. It was still under our bench a few minutes ago."

The boys retrieved it.

"What say we return this to Parks tomorrow?"

"You bet."

They would have driven over that evening, but there was a school dance. Chet's attractive, dark-haired sister Iola was going with Joe, and pretty, blond Callie Shaw with Frank.

Sunday afternoon the brothers looked up Parks's address in the telephone directory, then drove to Hopkinsville.

"There's the house, Frank," his brother called out, as they came to a tree-shaded ranch-style dwelling.

The tall, good-looking ballplayer answered the door.

"Hello, Parks," Joe greeted him.

"Joe and Frank Hardy!" George replied. "Come in. Say, I'll never forget you fellows after yesterday's game."

"It sure was close," Frank said.

"What brings you fellows to Hopkinsville?"

"We're returning some of your property." Frank held out a bag containing the moccasin.

"Thanks," he said, after Frank had explained about finding the moccasin. "I hated to lose that. Those loafers are the most comfortable shoes I own. I had to wear my football shoes home."

Taking off their overcoats, Frank and Joe quickly outlined their special reason for coming and pointed to the R mark inside the moccasin.

"What we want to know," said Frank, "is where you bought the moccasins."

"Golly, fellows," George replied quickly, "I know where *I* got them, but I can't tell you where they were purchased."

"You didn't buy them yourself?" Joe asked.

"Right. My uncle gave them to me as a present for my birthday last spring. All I know is that the moccasins were made by an Indian tribe. But what tribe I couldn't tell you," he concluded.

"Could you find out, George? It's important. It may help to catch a thief!"

"Good night!" Parks exclaimed. "That's right. You fellows are detectives, aren't you? Well, my uncle lives a couple of blocks from here. I'll ask him."

He went to the phone, but the line was busy, so he suggested that they walk over to see his uncle, who lived only a few blocks away. George's Uncle Ben was intrigued by the Hardys' story of their quest for the maker of the leather goods who used the mark R.

"I remember those moccasins well," said George's uncle, drawing on his pipe. "I bought them from a stranger on a train. I never saw him before, and I've never seen him since."

"An Indian?" Frank asked.

"No."

"Did he mention the name of the tribe?"

Uncle Ben shook his head. "No, the man didn't mention the name of the tribe—just said he'd bought them from an Indian and that they were too small for him."

The Hardys thanked the two Parks and started back to Bayport.

"It looks as though we're up a blind alley again. All of our clues lead us nowhere," Frank muttered.

"You know," his brother said thoughtfully, "if that marks means anything, the name of the tribe must begin with an R. Maybe we ought to do some research on Indians."

"Good idea," Frank agreed. "I wonder," he added thoughtfully, "if Breck can be an Indian."

"He didn't look like a full-blooded one."

"No, I meant a half-breed."

"I'll settle for a quarter."

Presently a familiar house came into view.

"Let's stop at Chet Morton's," Joe suggested. "I'm getting hungry, anyway."

Chet and Iola were home. Iola was mixing a batch of waffles under her brother's direction.

"We're just in time." Joe grinned. "Hope you've got plenty."

"Sure," Chet answered. "Iola, make twice as much batter. That'll be enough for a starter."

"I don't know about that," replied his sister teasingly. "Perhaps I'd better mix three times as much."

The chunky football center was known for his appetite, and despite needling from his friends, never reduced his intake of food.

Supper was a jolly affair but eventually the talk got around to the mystery in hand. Frank told of the slim clue they had picked up from the Parks.

He concluded the story by telling them that the moccasin had been made by an Indian tribe. As he was saying, "If only we knew the name of a tribe that begins with R," Iola and Chet looked at each other strangely.

"You know of one?" Joe asked.

"N-no," Chet replied, and in a moment disappeared from the room.

The Hardys continued to eat waffles with syrup.

Suddenly, as Joe got up to get more butter from the refrigerator, he gave a strangled cry. Frank turned to see what had startled his brother.

Standing in the doorway was an Indian in battle regalia!

CHAPTER VI

Buried Treasure

THE INDIAN raised his hand commandingly. Then a deep but strangely familiar voice intoned: "I am Chief Wallapatookunk."

"Chet!" whooped the Hardys, roaring with laughter as they recognized the voice.

"Where in the world did you get that Indian costume?" Frank asked.

Chet himself was struggling to maintain a dignified and fierce look.

"This Indian warrior's suit," he replied solemnly. "Chief say you his prisoners." He pointed to Iola. "Bring um white girl to Wallapatookunk."

Iola now was giggling but pretended to be alarmed and shrank toward Joe.

"I will defend this maiden to the last arrow!" Joe said, then added, "Have a heart, Chet, before I die laughing. Where did you get that Indian costume?"

"Long time ago in battle Chief Wallapa—Wallapa—" Chet tried to continue the masquerade but failed.

He gave a great guffaw as he yanked off his elaborate headdress.

"It's this way, fellows," Chet began, pulling out a handkerchief and wiping some of the red, black, and white crayon from his face. "My great-grandfather was a member of the Pashunk tribe."

"What!" Frank cried.

"You can't kid us, Chet," Joe admonished. "Everybody knows the Mortons have no Indian blood. Besides, your great-grandfather lived right here in Bayport," the young detective pointed out.

"Honest Injun, fellows," Chet insisted, "my great-grandfather belonged to the Pashunk tribe."

"He's right," Iola chimed in. The brothers, knowing Chet's sister to be serious-minded, listened with growing interest. "Yes, it's really true," she went on. "Great-grandfather was actually a member of an Indian tribe."

"Then I take it all back," Joe said. "So one of your ancestors was an Indian," he added with great respect.

Chet shook his head. "Not an Indian. But Great-grandfather Ezekiel Morton was honorary Chief Wallapatookunk of the Pashunks. This getup I'm wearing is a ceremonial outfit used only on special occasions. It's been in our family for generations, and I just thought of it again when you mentioned those Indian moccasins."

"What does Wallapatookunk mean?" Frank asked.

"Gee, fellows," Chet stammered, "you really don't want to know, do you?"

"We certainly do," Frank insisted.

"Well, it means 'Eat-a-Whole-Moose,' " Chet answered reluctantly.

"Boy, your great-grandfather must have had some appetite. Say, why didn't your folks call you Ezekiel?"

"Whoever heard of a center called Ezekiel?" Chet countered, ignoring the gibe.

"We don't know exactly how our great-grandfather got the Indian name," Iola spoke up, "but we do know a very strange legend that he used to tell. It has been handed down in our family and we never tire of hearing it."

"What's the legend?" Joe asked eagerly.

"The story goes like this," Chet began, then stopped. He looked around, obviously enjoying his role as narrator.

"Go on!"

"According to the legend we've been told, in the territory where the Pashunks used to live—the tribe died out years ago—let's see . . . How long ago was it, Iola?"

His listeners knew he was prolonging the story in order to needle the Hardys.

"Hey, Chet," protested Joe. "Enough of this suspense."

"Well, never mind," Chet went on. "Anyway, in that vicinity a fabulous treasure is buried!"

"Buried treasure!" The brothers whistled in amazement.

"Where is it buried?" Joe asked eagerly.

"No one knows."

"No one knows?" Frank echoed. "But there must be some clue."

"Yes, there is a single clue," Chet assented. "The legend says the treasure is buried in a crisscross shadow!"

"A crisscross shadow! The shadow of what?" Joe asked.

"That's what we don't know, but I sure wish you fellows would find the treasure for me," Chet concluded.

"For you?" Joe cried in mock indignation. "That's ducky. I can't think of anything in the world I'd rather do than find that buried treasure for you. I guess you'd like it dug up and sent special delivery, too!"

"And why not?" Chet complained. "After all, I'm a direct descendant of Chief Wallapa—"

Just then the doorbell rang and Iola excused herself to answer it. Meanwhile, Chet sat down to prepare more waffles.

"Hi, Frank! Hello, Joe! Chet! What in the world!"

cried a startled feminine voice as Callie Shaw saw the
boy's costume and his multicolored streaked face.

"Callie," Joe said solemnly, with a sweep of his
arm. "Let me present Great Chief Walla—er—any-
how, heap big wheel among Indians!"

Callie, though still puzzled, joined the outburst of
laughter at Joe's introduction of the disguised Chet.

Then, as Frank helped Callie take off her coat, he
brought her up to date on news in the Morton house-
hold and also what he and Joe had learned at Hopkinsville.

"You've really made progress in your detecting,"
Callie commented. "If you could only find out something further about that R imprint."

"Say, why don't we get out some of our collection
of old Indian books, Chet?" Iola spoke up. "Maybe
we'll find the name of some tribes that begin
with R."

"And then we'll check on whether they're the ones
who do leatherwork," Frank added enthusiastically.
"That's a wonderful idea, Iola."

Iola excused herself and returned a few minutes
later with an armload of old volumes.

"Here we are," she announced, and distributed a
few books to each one.

Immediately all the young people started thumb-
ing through the books, intently scanning the fine
print. The pages were yellowed and fragile with age.
Once in a while the searchers would come across a

name of a tribe in the same general locale, but on closer inspection it turned out to be one that began with a B or a G instead of an R.

There were dozens of tribes that no longer existed —names that had meant so much in the early days of the country—Abnakis, Shawnees, Narragansetts, and others that reminded the Bayport High students of the exciting days of the early colonists.

"This tribe we're looking for is probably so small that it didn't even make history," remarked Joe, breaking the studious silence. Everyone nodded agreement, but kept on leafing the pages determinedly.

But there was not a single small tribe that began with an R!

Finally it was time for the Hardys to start home, as they did not wish to break football training rules. Frank rode with Callie as far as her house, with Joe following, then transferred to the convertible.

"I guess we're at the end of the Indian trail with that moccasin," Joe remarked.

"Maybe the R tribe will turn up yet," Frank said more hopefully. "I'm not saying quits yet."

"I'm with you on that score," Joe agreed, as they turned the corner near the Hardy home.

Suddenly Frank gave a start and sat bolt upright. "Look!" he whispered excitedly. "Coming out of that window!"

Joe followed his brother's gaze to the second floor

of the Hardy house. In the moonlight they could see a man climbing out!

Frank cut the engine and stopped at the curb. The boys leaped from the car and raced up the driveway.

As they looked up again, the intruder was dropping to the roof of the kitchen porch. Then a cloud hid the scene in darkness.

"Come on! He mustn't get away!" Frank cried.

In the darkness the boys heard a thud on the ground. They reached the porch just as the moon broke through the clouds.

They could see no one!

In the second that the clouds had obscured the moon, the intruder had disappeared as if the earth had swallowed him up!

CHAPTER VII

Fouled Up

WHERE had the man who had climbed out the second-story window gone? Frank and Joe immediately went into action.

"Quick!" said Joe to his brother. "I'll circle this side of the house. You take the other."

Finding no one, they searched neighboring yards. It was no use. The man had disappeared.

"Let's go inside and see if he took anything," Frank urged.

Noticing that several lights had been turned on upstairs, the boys dashed up to the second floor.

"Who's there? What do you want?" their mother's agitated voice called out.

"It's Frank and Joe," Frank called back. "Are you all right?" he asked anxiously.

"Oh, boys, what a relief to see you!" Mrs. Hardy cried as they reached the hall.

But Aunt Gertrude stood menacingly, an umbrella clutched in her hand.

"You boys!" she exclaimed. "Why'd you have to stay out so late? You know your mother and I are here alone. Never around when we need you. Detectives, are you? You should have been here a few minutes sooner. Then you'd have had a real mystery on your hands."

"Yes, we know," Frank replied quickly. "We saw the man crawling out of the second-story window."

"Then why didn't you catch him?" Aunt Gertrude bristled.

"We tried," Frank confessed, "but he got away."

"Did he steal anything?" Joe put in. "Did you see him?"

"See him?" echoed Aunt Gertrude with indignation. "We saw him, and I've never been more scared in my life! If I ever get that fellow, I'll turn him over my knee and give him the thrashing of his life."

Their aunt's eyes flashed. It was obvious that if she ever got her hands on the interloper she would do just as she had threatened.

"I'll explain," said Mrs. Hardy. "Aunt Gertrude and I came home from the movies. When we got upstairs we thought we heard a noise in your father's study."

"That's the room he was climbing out of," Frank said excitedly.

"We looked in there," the boys' mother went on,

"and saw a masked man. As soon as he saw us, he dived for the window and climbed out."

"I tried to grab him," Aunt Gertrude put in. "But he pushed me away and threw me to the floor, the beast!"

Frank and Joe became furious as they visualized the scene.

"What was the man doing when you saw him?" Frank asked.

"He was standing before your father's file cabinet and he had a key in his hand!"

"He was trying to open the cabinet!" Joe exclaimed.

As the women nodded, the boys rushed into their father's study and examined the file carefully. Apparently it had not been disturbed. Getting the new key, Frank opened it. The contents seemed to be intact.

"Good thing we changed that lock," Joe said.

"Right. But the criminal might have forced it open." He turned to his mother and Aunt Gertrude. "I guess you frightened him off in time."

"I wonder what that man was after," Joe pondered.

"It could be most anything," Frank replied thoughtfully. "Let's fine-tooth comb this room. Maybe the fellow unwittingly left a clue that may help us track him down."

They examined the study from wall to wall but found nothing. As Joe leaned against the cabinet, a disappointed frown on his face, suddenly something caught his eye. Reaching down, he pulled at a bit of wool snagged on the corner of one drawer.

"We missed this," he said. "Oh, boy, what a clue!"

Triumphantly he flashed a strand of royal-blue wool! "That man in the house in Southport! Remember? He was wearing a royal-blue sweater!"

"Correct." Frank beamed. "Now we're beginning to get somewhere on this case! Aunt Gertrude, you said the burglar had a key in his hand. I'll bet anything it was the key to this cabinet!"

"Sure," agreed Joe. "And that proves Breck *did* take the key. After he skipped Bayport, either he or his lawyer gave it to the man in the royal-blue sweater. He came here tonight."

"Maybe those two guys who slugged us in that Southport tenement house were Breck and Kamp!" Frank reasoned. "They were just arriving to give Mr. Blue Sweater the key."

"Everything ties together," Joe nodded in satisfaction. "But the important question's still not answered. What did this gang want from Dad's file so badly that they went to so much trouble to get the key?"

"Let's go back to Southport tomorrow and call on that sweater guy again," Frank proposed.

Since the football squad was excused from practice on Monday, the Hardys were able to start for Southport as soon as classes were over.

"How about coming along, Chet?" Frank said as they got ready to leave.

"Sorry, fellows. I promised Dad I'd clean the chicken coop. But listen, you two, don't get yourselves in the hospital. We've got a tough game to play on Saturday and—"

"Where you fellows going?" Tony Prito spoke up. "Maybe I can be your bodyguard."

"Swell."

The three boys drove to the dock where their small powerboat the *Sleuth* was moored. They would make the trip to Southport by water across Eagle Bay.

Arriving at the dock, the trio leaped into the *Sleuth* and cast off.

"Okay, Frank. Give 'er all she's got," Joe urged.

The *Sleuth* skimmed across Eagle Bay while the trio chatted about school and football. Suddenly Frank exclaimed:

"Uh, uh, something's wrong with the rudder!"

He throttled the engine, and while it idled, Joe and Tony tinkered with the rudder.

"It's jammed!" Joe called out.

The *Sleuth* drifted with the tide, slapped and spanked by the choppy water. The rudder would not budge.

"We're headed straight for Merriam Island!" Frank shouted.

Ahead lay the rocky islet on which a famous lighthouse stood. The light was a warning to mariners to keep away from the treacherous rocks. Nevertheless there had been many wrecks there. Soon the rocky promontory was only fifty yards off the bow.

"Let's jump!" Tony cried out. "She's going to crash!"

"Put 'er in reverse!" Joe shouted.

Frank started the engine and threw the clutch into reverse. But the *Sleuth* merely spun around, still helpless without the rudder!

In desperation, Frank gave the engine more gas. The propeller churned the water into foam. Then suddenly the cable rudder loosened. Frank swung the *Sleuth* in a sharp turn, missing the jagged shore by inches.

"Whew!" said Tony. "That was too close to be funny."

"I'll say." Joe whistled.

Frank was quiet but his heart was pounding. With a sigh of relief he headed for Southport again.

"The *Sleuth* never acted this way before," remarked Joe. "I wonder what ails her."

Whatever the ailment had been, it was over now, for the rest of the trip was uneventful. Frank nudged the craft into a dock near the house where the Hardys had had their earlier adventure.

"Say, there's a cradle over there." He pointed. "Let's put the *Sleuth* in there and see if everything's okay."

Joe went to ask the owner of the boat cradle if they might use it, then waved Frank in. As soon as the *Sleuth* was out of water, the boys examined the rudder and cable leading to it.

"Here's the trouble," Joe said, holding up a piece of loose wire. "Our rudder was fouled!"

"I see what happened," Frank said. "A coil of wire was stuffed in there. After a while it wound itself tight around the cable where the rudder's attached."

"Do you think somebody wanted to keep you away from Southport?" Tony asked.

"Could be," Frank replied. "But it could be just an accident, too. After all, there's a lot of refuse floating around the water front."

"Refuse and bad characters," said Joe, "making the water front a good place to look for our enemies."

"Correct. And we're going after one of them right now."

The boys put the *Sleuth* back in the water and asked Tony to guard it while they were gone.

"Sure." He grinned. "And I'll try to pick up one or two of those enemies while I'm waiting."

The Hardys headed up a steep cobblestone alley to the street and walked in the main entrance of the water-front tenement where Philip York lived.

Joe rapped on the apartment door, while Frank kept an eye on the dim corridor to avoid another surprise attack.

The door was opened by the man they had come to see. He was wearing the telltale blue sweater.

"What do you want?" he asked roughly.

"To talk to you."

The man's eyes widened when he recognized his callers. "You boys are going to get hurt coming around here," he said threateningly. "I can't give you any information."

"Oh, no?" retorted Joe skeptically, then shot the question, "What were you doing in our house last night?"

"Your house? I've never been near the place in my life," York replied angrily.

"That's your story," Frank spoke up. "Here, take a look at this," he said, forcing his way in and suddenly confronting the man with the piece of blue yarn. "It came from that sweater you're wearing," he declared accusingly, pointing to a tear in the front of it.

The man looked blank, then recovered. "Maybe it did, maybe it didn't. Anyway, it ain't my sweater," he said defensively. "I borrowed it from another guy."

"We don't believe you," Frank answered firmly. Both boys were in the room now. "You'd better start talking."

"I won't tell you a thing," York replied. But his voice had lost some of its confidence. His eyes shifted from one boy to the other nervously.

"Look, fellows," he said meekly, "take it easy on a guy that ain't to blame, will you? I'll do anything you ask. You've got the goods on me."

The Hardys had not expected to get a confession this easily. They looked at each other with satisfaction. At last they were making headway on the case!

CHAPTER VIII

An Elusive Suspect

THE SUSPECT continued to babble and to say he would tell them everything he knew.

"Then come along to the police station with us," Frank said sternly. "They'll want to hear what you have to say."

"Okay," the man replied, rubbing his hands together nervously. "Right away?"

"Yes."

"I'll have to get my coat out of the bedroom. I'll only be a minute," he told them shakily. "You wait here."

Before they could object, the man turned, went into an adjoining room, and closed the door. The boys exchanged glances.

"I wonder what made him change his mind so quickly," Joe whispered.

"I think we'd better keep a close watch on him," Frank answered. "He may try to get away from us on the street."

"Yes," Joe agreed, and called out, "Say, you in there!"

There was no reply.

"Hurry up!" Frank ordered.

Still no response.

"We'd better see what he's up to!" Joe exclaimed, worried.

The boys burst into the room. Their eyes took in the shabbily furnished bedroom in a glance.

There was no one in sight!

"He's given us the slip!" Frank cried out.

"There's no way out except by the windows and they're locked from the inside," Joe replied. "He's got to be here somewhere!"

The boys began a careful search of the room. They looked under the bed, poked into a closet, even looking for a secret door in it, and tapped the wall for a hidden panel. But the man in the blue sweater had disappeared!

"There's only one place left," said Frank. "The floor."

No trap door was apparent, but when he crawled under the bed and felt around on the floor, he found one that opened downward.

"Here's how he got out!" Frank exclaimed. "Joe, you guard the hall and I'll go after him this way."

"Okay. Give our whistle if you want me to join you."

Frank squeezed through the opening onto a rope ladder which swung down from the edge of the trap door. In the dimness below, the young detective could see what looked like a floor.

"It must be the basement," he told himself, as he reached the end of the ladder and stepped on the hard surface.

The place had a musty, damp odor. The scraping of his feet echoed dismally in the dark room.

He whipped out his pocket flashlight and flicked it on.

No one was revealed.

"He may be hiding," Frank thought, as the beam picked up several barrels, some dust-covered furniture, and a few scattered trunks.

Inch by inch Frank went over the basement. But the man in the royal-blue sweater was not there.

"How you coming?" Joe called down.

"He got out of here somehow. There must be a door."

At that moment Frank heard a familiar sound—the put-put of a motorboat.

"This basement must be right close to the dock!" he shouted up to Joe.

His flashlight swept the walls of the room.

"Yes, I see a door, Joe. I'll let you know what happens."

He hurried over to the door, twisted the knob, and pushed. The door opened easily.

Blinking in the bright sunlight, Frank looked around.

He was standing alone on a small dock that poked its nose into Eagle Bay.

Where was York?

Joe was peering from the living-room window. Now he raised the sash and called:

"See anything?"

"Nothing but the *Sleuth*."

Joe looked toward where his brother pointed.

"Tony! Hey, Tony!" Frank shouted across to the next dock.

Their friend's head appeared over the stern. "Hello, I'll come and get you."

"Did you see anybody come out of here?" Frank called.

"Sure. A few minutes ago two men came out."

"Where'd they go?"

"They boarded a speedboat and headed off toward Bayport."

"Did one of them have on a blue sweater?"

"No. But come to think of it, one man had something blue rolled up under his arm."

"He's the guy we're looking for!" Frank exclaimed. "Joe, come on down! We're going after them!"

When Tony brought the *Sleuth* up, the boat shot out into Eagle Bay and headed for Bayport.

"I only hope this boat doesn't foul up again," Tony said, worried.

Scanning the bay, his hand shading his eyes from the sun, he suddenly shouted, "There they are, Frank. Give 'er the gun!"

The other motorboat was plowing through the choppy water at a fast clip. Frank turned on full speed and the *Sleuth* fairly leaped across the waves.

Fast as the fleeing boat was, the *Sleuth* was faster, and gradually the Hardys' craft began to close up the distance that separated them.

"We're gaining. We're catching up!" Tony exulted. He narrowed his eyes as he tried to make out the identity of the boat's occupants.

In a few moments the boys could see clearly two figures crouching in the stern and a third at the wheel.

"There's the fellow with the blue sweater, all right," Joe announced. "But he's masked now!"

"Say—the other fellow might be Breck," guessed Frank, gripping the wheel tensely.

"Could be," returned Tony, "but he's got a mask on, too."

"Can't tell yet who's at the wheel," put in Joe, straining his eyes to see. "Can't you get up more speed, Frank?"

"Got her as wide open as she'll go. We're still gaining, though. At this rate we'll overtake them in no time!"

Relentlessly the *Sleuth* plowed on, closer and closer to the fleeing craft. Finally Frank narrowed the gap between them to about a hundred yards and began to edge in toward the boat ahead.

"York's trying to hide!" yelled Tony as he discerned the figure hunched over in the rear seat. Just then the man beside him jerked his head around toward the pursuers and shouted something to the pilot of the fleeing speedboat.

Instantly the craft swerved sharply to the left. But just as swiftly Frank turned the *Sleuth* in the same direction.

From then on it was a zigzag chase. The fugitive boat, veering crazily from side to side, churned the water to such a froth it was almost enveloped in spray.

Nevertheless, the *Sleuth* clung to the course, and Joe shouted encouragingly:

"Atta boy, Frank! They're just trying to shake us. Stick to 'em!"

With that he made a megaphone of his hands. "Stop!" he cried. "That tricky business won't do you any good. You can't get away from us!"

York's companion turned around. Standing up, he shouted back:

"Scram outta here, you fool kids!"

The man at the wheel resumed a straight course. No longer did he swerve the boat, but pursued a beeline for Bayport.

The *Sleuth* roared up behind the speedboat. It was Frank's intention to get alongside and try persuading the man with the sweater to give up.

Suddenly the runaway's companion bent down. As he straightened up, he raised a heavy log of wood and heaved it. The log soared through the air, directly in the path of the onrushing *Sleuth*.

"Frank! Look out!" Joe cried.

Frank swung the wheel with all his might. But it was too late. With a splintering crash the *Sleuth* violently rammed the log!

CHAPTER IX

A Brush with the Enemy

THE SHOCK of the collision was so violent that the boys were catapulted from the *Sleuth* into the cold water of Eagle Bay.

In a few seconds three heads emerged from the waves.

"Joe! Tony!" Frank shouted out. "Are you all right?"

"Okay, here!" Joe called.

"I'm all right, too," Tony answered.

To their amazement the *Sleuth* was still afloat, drifting aimlessly some yards away. As the three boys swam to it, they noticed that an immense hole had been torn in her bow at the water line.

"She's going to sink!" Tony cried woefully.

They clambered aboard and Frank discovered that the impact had switched off the engine. When he tried to start it, there was not a sound. It was dead!

"This is a fine pickle," he said in disgust.

"Where did the other boat go?" Tony asked anxiously.

The boys scanned the bay, but could see only a cluster of small craft near the shore. The men had made good their escape!

"They've sure disappeared into thin air," remarked Joe.

"Yeah," Tony commented. "That log thrower did the trick for 'em."

"There's one clue, though, that they've given us," Frank put in. "Did you notice that huge scar on his hand before he tossed the log at us?"

"Say—that's right!" exclaimed Joe. "I did see it. It was W-shaped, too! That means it was probably our friend Breck!"

"We practically had him!" Frank groaned. "Fine time to be stuck like this."

"And we're drifting with the tide," Tony pointed out as he noticed the shore line receding.

Half an hour later Tony gave a shout and motioned toward a low-slung cabin cruiser that was bearing down on them.

"Look, fellows, isn't that the Coast Guard cutter *Mallimuk?*"

"You're right!" Joe exclaimed.

The three boys shouted and waved their arms to signal the cutter. The captain saw them and drew alongside. When Frank explained the reason for their predicament, Captain Barnes shook his head in anger.

"I'll send out an alarm for those men right away," he assured them. "Meanwhile, we'll give you and the *Sleuth* a lift home."

While he radioed headquarters, a guardsman threw a line from the cutter. Joe fastened it to the *Sleuth*, and the damaged craft was towed to its dock in Bayport.

The boys thanked the men and went to their car. After dropping Tony off at his house, they made arrangements to have the boat repaired, then drove home. Mrs. Hardy was waiting anxiously, a worried look on her face.

"Mother," Joe asked, "is something the matter?"

"Yes, boys, there is," she replied. "It's Sam Radley. He's been injured!"

"Gee, that's a shame," Joe said.

"What happened, Mother?" Frank asked. "One of the saboteurs get him?"

"Yes. Sam caught up with a suspect and they had a tussle. The man got away, but Sam was thrown and broke his leg."

"Where is he now?"

"In Bayport Hospital."

"We'd better go and see him right away," Frank declared.

The brothers drove off immediately and were at the hospital in a few moments. They found their father's associate with his left leg in a plaster cast.

"We're sorry about this," Joe said. "How do you feel now?"

"Pretty well, boys," came the reply. "But I sure hated to lose my man."

"What happened?" Frank asked.

Briefly, Sam Radley told them he had received a tip to look along the water front for certain characters and had trapped one of the suspects in a boathouse outside Bayport. While he was taking him to his car, the man had made a break for it. In the fracas that followed, the saboteur had pushed Sam into a deep ditch. The detective pointed to his cast.

"This was the result."

"At least you're making headway on the case," Joe remarked.

"I *was*." Sam smiled ruefully. "This sets me back. But without question your father and I are getting closer to cracking the case. On the other hand, the saboteurs are becoming bolder. They're likely to strike anywhere, any time!"

"Gosh," Joe expostulated, "I hope you'll get them soon before they do any real damage." Then he asked, "Sam, what did the man who escaped look like?"

"He's heavy built," the assistant detective replied. "Dark-haired and swarthy-complexioned."

Frank leaned forward tensely as he heard this description.

"Were there any distinguishing marks on this man that you tussled with?" he asked.

"Yes. He has a large W-shaped scar on the back of his right hand."

"Scar on the back of his hand!" Frank exclaimed, and told of their recent adventures. "The man who threw the log at our boat had a scar—a W-shaped one—on the back of his right hand. And what's more," he continued eagerly, "Breck, the phony leather goods salesman, had the same scar on *his* hand. I'll bet that Breck, the man in the boat, and the saboteur are all the same person!"

"You're right," Joe agreed.

Sam Radley stroked his chin thoughtfully and looked down at his injured leg. "Maybe you'll catch him before I do. Keep your eyes open and your wits about you. Those fellows are dangerous. The one who got away from me is known as Killer Johnson."

"Was he hiding in the boathouse or did he come there in a boat?" Joe asked.

"He was just coming out of it as I came along," Sam answered. "I didn't see a boat bring him, though."

The boys talked a few moments more with Sam, then said good-by, promising to watch for clues that might help on the sabotage case.

On the way home Joe said, "I wonder where that boat disappeared to after the log was thrown at us?"

"There are a lot of little coves and inlets along the

shore that it could have ducked into without being seen," his brother replied.

"Maybe we ought to search along the shore," Joe suggested.

After several hours of fruitless searching of the shore line along the bay, the boys turned homeward.

"Those fellows probably pulled out of town. They may have seen the Coast Guard pick us up. I'm sure that after they dropped Breck they went into hiding," Frank pointed out.

"I think our best bet right now is to follow up the clue of the moccasin," said Joe. "It's a clue to the real identity of Breck and might lead us to his pals."

"No doubt about it—that's the best method of attack," his brother agreed.

When the boys arrived home they found Aunt Gertrude sitting on the porch.

"Golly, I'm hungry. What's for supper, Aunt Gertrude?" Frank asked.

"Fricasseed chicken and all the trimmings," she announced.

"Trimmings?" Joe repeated. "You mean feathers and everything? Why, Auntie!"

His relative withered his teasing with a disdainful look and led the way to the dining room.

During the meal, the boys told her and their mother about Sam Radley's condition and their suspicion that he had been after the same man they were.

"I guess we'll have to do Sam's work," Frank observed with a sidewise look at his aunt, knowing she would object.

"Sam's work, indeed!" she cried. "You leave the saboteurs to the big detectives!"

"Tall, you mean? I'm as tall as Sam."

"Now, boys," Mrs. Hardy cautioned, hoping the banter would not get out of hand.

"Solving crimes certainly gives them a good appetite for food and wit," Aunt Gertrude observed as each was served a third dumpling.

"You'll be sorry for both."

The Hardy boys groaned at the thought of more food when dessert arrived, but Aunt Gertrude's chocolate nut cake was a special favorite of theirs. When they finished a generous helping, the young sleuths leaned back with a sigh.

"Aunt Gertrude," said Joe, "sometimes I'd rather eat one of your meals than solve a mystery!"

It was the highest compliment her nephew could pay her and Miss Hardy blushed. At that moment the telephone rang. Mrs. Hardy, who was nearest the instrument, answered it.

"Joe! Frank!" she called. "It's Iola Morton and Callie Shaw. You'd better hurry. They seem excited!"

"Gosh," said Joe, his eyebrows rising in puzzlement. "I wonder what's up now."

Reaching the phone, Frank picked it up. "Hello,

Iola . . . Callie?" he asked anxiously. "What's the trouble?"

"Hello, Frank." It was Iola. "Callie and I have been looking through some more Indian books and we've come across something important."

"What is it?"

"We've found the name of an Indian tribe that begins with an R!"

Frank whistled in amazement. "Great work, Iola. What's the name?"

"The Ramapans."

"Ramapans?" Frank repeated. "Listen, we'll be right over."

Twenty minutes later the Hardys arrived at the Mortons.

"Hi, everybody!" Joe greeted Callie, Chet, and Iola. "What's this about an Indian tribe?"

"Iola and I decided we'd look through some more books on Indians that Chet remembered were in the attic," Callie explained. "We'd just about given up our search when we came across some information about the Ramapans."

"That's great," said Joe. "Where are they located and what are they like?"

He pulled out a notebook and pencil ready to take down all the information.

"Well, the Ramapans are a small tribe. They live on a reservation about five hundred miles from here," Callie replied.

"Yes. Go on," Frank urged eagerly as the girl paused.

"They are skilled in making small trinkets and leather articles."

"Skilled in leatherwork!" Frank exclaimed.

"I thought that would make you sit up and take notice." Chet grinned. "Just come to Morton and Company for the best in detecting."

"We have our clue to the moccasin!" Joe cried.

"Sure you have."

"Can you show us on the map where the Ramapans live?" Frank asked.

Chet brought out an atlas and opened it. After turning several pages, he pointed.

"Here it is. Not many people live around that region."

The Hardys recognized the area as rugged territory made up mostly of mountains and forest.

"Say," Chet called out suddenly, "that's right around where the Pashunks used to live!"

"The Ramapans and the Pashunks in the same area!" Joe whistled.

Chet's face lit up with expectation. "Fellows," he said, "I have a wonderful idea. Let's go there and search for that buried treasure!"

CHAPTER X

A Lucky Break

"NEAT idea, eh?" Chet said enthusiastically. "I could use some of that treasure right now. A little matter of a few bills I owe."

"Sure, it's a great idea, Chet," Frank replied. "But the Ramapans might not agree. They own the land where their reservation is located. And you've forgotten something else—school. How would you get time off from classes?"

"Well, maybe if we called it a science expedition—"

"That's a better idea, Chet." Joe grinned. "But I'm afraid we never could sell it to the principal."

"And even if we could, how about the football games?" Frank asked. "Bayport High might get along without Joe and me, but our big center—no!"

Chet beamed at the compliment.

"Right now, we have a mystery to solve," Joe said.

"And we do have a good clue to the maker of the

key case and the moccasin, and that's pretty important right now," Frank added.

The young people spent the rest of the evening poring over the story of the Ramapans, learning their history and customs. As the Hardys were leaving, Frank said:

"I certainly hope we can put all this knowledge to some good use."

Next afternoon, between the end of classes and football practice, he and Joe dropped in to see Chief Collig and ask if there was any news from the Southport police about Breck and the man in the blue sweater.

"Nothing good," the officer replied, leaning back in his swivel chair. "They've disappeared—at least for the time being. But a twelve-state alarm has been sent out for them."

"But don't worry, boys," the chief went on encouragingly. "Those two will turn up again, and when they do, they'll be arrested."

Frank looked at his watch. "Well, it's time to get over to football practice. Thanks for the information, Chief."

During the next two hours they worked hard, running, tackling, trying out signals under the watchful eye of Coach Devlin. Finally, when the sun was setting over the empty stands, he dismissed the squad, telling them to take one lap around the field before hitting the showers.

The brothers trotted along side by side. Joe, his face streaked with dirt and perspiration from the hard workout, mopped his brow with the sleeve of his jersey.

"You know," he said, "I'd like to follow up the key-case clue in the Ramapan country right away. We might fly up there for the week end."

"That wouldn't be time enough to make a thorough investigation," his brother pointed out. "How about Christmas vacation?"

"Gosh, Frank, I'd hate to wait until Christmas to call on the Ramapans. But maybe we'll figure out a way."

After dinner that evening Frank and Joe turned to their homework. "Getting an education's all right," Joe sighed, "but I'd rather be hunting for Breck or York."

"Me, too," Frank agreed. "But right now I've got to concentrate on algebra."

When the brothers arrived at school next morning, a crowd of boys and girls were gathered around the main entrance to the building. The Hardys hurried up, curious to find out what was going on. Usually, students lingered outside for only a moment, then went to their classes. Seeing their friend Biff Hooper in the group, Frank and Joe walked over to him.

"Hi, Biff!" Frank greeted the rangy fullback. "What's all the excitement?"

"Have a look for yourself," Biff replied, pointing to a sign tacked on the entrance.

The boys edged over for a closer look, but knew from the animated conversation around them what it said.

"Because of a breakdown in the heating plant, all classes and sports have been suspended temporarily. You will be advised over the radio when school will reopen."

"'Classes suspended!'" repeated Frank. He whistled in astonishment.

"Pretty neat, eh?" Biff said delightedly. "Now I'll have time to work on that sailboat I'm building for next summer."

Joe's face broke into a wide grin. "One guess, Frank, what we'll do with the time."

"Go up to the Ramapan country!"

"Right. Come on. Let's tell Chet. He'll probably want to come along and hunt for that buried treasure!"

Their stout friend, who never reached school until the very last minute, arrived at that moment in his rattling jalopy. The boys met him at the curb.

"What! No school! Do I want to go!" he exclaimed when he heard the news. "Yippee!"

"Okay, Chet, let's go to the station and find out about trains," Frank suggested.

The agent informed them that a through train for

Lantern Junction, the nearest village to the Ramapans, stopped at Bayport at eleven o'clock.

"Don't be late!" Frank warned Chet as he dropped them at their house. "Remember, we don't have all day to make that train—just a couple of hours!"

"Say, whose treasure is this, anyway?" Chet called, as the jalopy shuddered violently from the meshing of gears. "I'm practically at the station now!" And the ancient car lurched and clattered down the street.

Reaching home, Frank and Joe told their mother and Aunt Gertrude about the heating-plant breakdown and their plan to visit the Ramapans.

Mrs. Hardy was somewhat taken aback by their announcement of the proposed trip. But she resolved not to voice the anxiety she felt.

"Take plenty of warm clothes," she advised. "It's very cold up there at this time of year. And I'll get some money for you."

When she left the room Aunt Gertrude tapped her fingers on a table. "The idea of closing the school and not making you study!" she said.

As her nephews grinned broadly at this statement, she continued in a firm tone, "If I were the principal I'd give you plenty of homework so you couldn't go gallivanting off to talk to a lot of Indians!"

"Zingo! I'm glad I never had you for a teacher, Auntie!" Joe cried. "Tell you what! We'll bring you back a nice scalp for a souvenir."

He fled upstairs before she could reply, Frank following. They had barely started pulling out ski clothes when their aunt came into their room.

"Shoo!" she ordered. "I'll do the packing. What do you know about it anyway—nothing. Go get your bags," Aunt Gertrude directed crisply. "Then leave me alone."

"Don't worry. We will," Joe agreed cheerfully. "There's no better packer in Bayport."

At this moment Mrs. Hardy entered the room. "Here's a letter for you boys," she said, handing it to Joe. "A boy brought it."

"Thanks, Mom." He studied the envelope for a moment.

"Who's it from?" Frank asked.

"I don't know," Joe replied. "There's no return address and the handwriting's not familiar."

He ripped open the plain white envelope. As he read the message his eyes widened in surprise and a strange expression came over his face. He gave the letter to his brother without a word. Frank's eyebrows shot up at the warning it held:

"Don't meddle. Stay home if you value your life. R."

CHAPTER XI

Secret Writing

"WHAT is it?" Mrs. Hardy asked.

"Yes, something mighty peculiar's going on, judging from the look on your faces," Aunt Gertrude told her nephews. "Own up!"

Frank read the note aloud. The women gasped, and instantly thought the boys should abandon the trip.

"But, Mother," Frank said, "I'm sure Dad would want us to carry through. If we told him someone was trying to get his secret papers and didn't follow it up, he wouldn't think much of us as detectives."

"Nevertheless—"

"Of course," Joe said, "if you and Aunt Gertrude are afraid to stay alone—"

"Such talk!" Their aunt bristled. "Didn't I chase that burglar away singlehanded?"

Finally, consent to the trip was given and the packing went on. Frank and Joe left the room. Out in the hall Frank whispered:

"I guess that Breck or York must have been spying on us and heard our plans."

"Yes, and those fellows really mean business."

Frank set his jaw. "That makes us even. You and I meant business all along. And now that we know we're dealing with a gang that's desperate, it'll be all the more exciting tracking them down. Right now, what say we take this note to Chief Collig and have it analyzed for fingerprints, etc. We haven't time to do it."

"Okay. Let's get moving. We don't want to miss that train."

When the boys arrived at police headquarters, the desk sergeant greeted them with a friendly hello. "Say, you fellows are getting to be regulars here. Chief Collig's in his office. Go right in."

When they entered, it was obvious from their faces that they did not bring a good report.

"Good morning," the chief said. "What's on your minds? Bad news?"

Frank handed him the letter and told him about their coming trip. Chief Collig turned from a pile of rogues' gallery photographs he had been examining, a grave expression on his face.

"Sounds as if trouble's brewing for you two," he commented soberly. "I wish your dad were here to advise you."

"We'll be all right," Frank assured the officer.

The chief's big hands fumbled with the envelope as he drew out the folded paper inside. A look of bewilderment crossed his ruddy face.

"Boys," he said, looking directly at them, "are you playing a trick on me? This paper is blank."

"Blank!" Frank cried out, seizing the letter.

To his complete amazement, the white sheet of paper had absolutely nothing on it!

"Chief Collig," Frank declared in embarrassment, "I'll swear there was a message on this paper only fifteen minutes ago."

Joe, astounded, could only nod in agreement.

The chief spread his palms and smiled. "I don't know what to say, boys. I'd hate to think you'd play a trick like this on an old duffer like me, but you can't expect me to take action on a threatening message if there is no message."

"Honestly, Chief," Joe insisted, "there was a threat written on this paper, telling us to stay away from the Ramapan country if we valued our lives."

The telephone rang. As the officer reached over to answer it, Frank nudged his brother.

"Come on, Joe, let's go home." He picked up the letter and envelope from the chief's desk, and called good-by to the officer.

Without questioning why, Joe followed Frank from headquarters. But out on the sidewalk he demanded an explanation.

"What's the big hurry?" he asked. "I thought we were going to ask the chief to examine the letter."

A knowing smile played over Frank's lips. "Ever hear of secret writing?" he asked quietly.

Joe slapped him on the back. "Of course. It's that ink that disappears a few minutes after the paper is exposed to light. Why didn't I think of that?"

"What we must do," Frank went on, "is restore the writing."

Arriving home, the boys hurried to their laboratory in the basement. Joe mixed a formula he had learned from his science teacher and applied it to the paper. Nothing happened.

"I guess the writing's gone for good." He sighed.

"Maybe not," Frank spoke up. "How about trying that new preparation Dad just developed for the FBI?"

"That's top-secret stuff," Joe said.

"Dad won't mind a bit," Frank replied. "He told me before he left that we could have full use of his lab."

The chemical was a purple-colored powder, which they sprinkled lightly over their letter.

"Now we put this in solution A and then solution B," Frank said.

"What are they?" Joe asked, puzzled.

"Only Dad and the government know that," his brother replied. "But here are the solutions."

Quickly the boys passed the letter through one

liquid, dried it with an electric fan, and then put it into the second solution.

Then faintly, as if by magic, the letters began to appear on the paper. Presently the whole message came into view, bold and legible.

"Great work, Frank. Now, let's rush this right back to Chief Collig before it disappears again."

The boys burst into his office a few minutes later and thrust the paper before the startled officer's eyes. Frank explained what they had done.

"Well, I take it all back," he apologized, and read the message in a glance. "This is serious," he declared, stroking his chin. "A dangerous gang to deal with. I warn you boys to keep on the alert every minute."

"We'll do that," Joe promised. "I want to hang around this planet a little longer."

Pointing to the envelope, Frank asked, "Don't you think a lab check of this letter would be in order, Chief Collig?"

"Right you are, Frank. Come on. We'll do it right away," he replied, beckoning them toward the police department's crime laboratory.

A check of the fingerprints on the letter did not tally with those of any known criminal, and there were no identifying marks to tell from whom the letter had come.

"It's not a whole sheet, and it's written on heavy paper, we know that much," Chief Collig determined. "I'd say it was cut from a long, narrow sheet."

Frank picked up the letter. "I wonder—" he began slowly, "I wonder if it could be *legal* paper." He held one edge of it to the light. "Yes, it is!" he exclaimed, seeing the semblance of a blue line where the paper had been cut.

"Fine deduction, Frank," the chief complimented him. "But what person who uses legal paper might be mixed up in this business?"

"Miles Kamp!"

"Of course!" the officer agreed. "He was Wylie Breck's lawyer!"

Picking up his telephone, the officer said, "Sergeant, I want two men detailed to watch Miles Kamp, the lawyer. Shadow him day and night and give me a full report on everything he does, where he goes, whom he sees."

He replaced the instrument in its cradle and turned to the Hardys.

"All right, boys. I think we're getting somewhere at last, thanks to you. That note tipped the gang's hand." He looked at his watch. "Don't miss your train. And good luck," he called as the boys went out the door.

They stopped at the house just long enough to collect their bags. Mrs. Hardy, who was going to a club meeting with Aunt Gertrude, drove them to the railroad station.

The platform was crowded, but the boys had no

trouble finding Chet Morton among the throng. He was surrounded by enough luggage to stay away a month.

"Changing to the Lantern Junction High School?" Joe needled his friend. "The squad'll sure miss you."

"Aw, cut it out," Chet begged. "That's rugged country, and a fellow can't be too well equipped."

The place seethed with young people, many of them friends of the boys who were taking advantage of the unexpected holiday to make sight-seeing trips.

"Where you going? Sleuthing?" Pete Williams called to the Hardys.

"You guessed it."

"Don't tell me you're helping 'em, Chet," Pete said, grinning.

"Sure. I'm going Injun hunting. One of 'em scalped my great-grandfather."

The laughter that followed this remark almost drowned out the whistle of the approaching train.

The three boys made their way to the edge of the platform to await its arrival. Chet leaned over the track to try to look around a bend beyond the station.

"Here she comes, fellows!" he cried, catching a glimpse of the engine.

The train came closer. As it turned the bend, a shrill scream from the street cut the air.

At the instant that everyone's attention was diverted, the Hardy boys suddenly felt themselves shoved toward the track by strong hands. They struggled against the pressure but were thrown off balance.

"You will horn in where you have no business to, will you?" a rasping voice muttered in Frank's ear.

"Stop!" Frank cried out.

But the plea was useless. Their arms flailing the air, both Hardy boys went tumbling off the platform directly into the path of the oncoming train!

CHAPTER XII

Conflicting Reports

THE TRAIN bore down on the Hardys who were sprawled across the track. Men shouted. Women screamed and covered their eyes. Train brakes shrieked.

Instinct made Frank rise instantly and jump back. But Joe was stunned, the breath knocked from him. Chet was the first onlooker to make a move. Quick as lightning he jumped down from the platform, lifted Joe, and stepped out of the path of the train as it rushed by them!

"Oh! Thank goodness!" someone cried out.

Still trembling, the brothers stood stock-still, unable to believe they had been saved. Then Joe looked at Chet and murmured:

"Thanks, pal."

As the train came to a stop, everyone excitedly began to talk at once. What had happened? Had the surge of the crowd pushed the boys onto the track? someone asked.

"No," Frank answered, recovering his wits. "We were shoved."

Just then the conductor rushed up to find out why the brakes had been jammed on so suddenly. He received a terse explanation of what had occurred, then Frank asked him to hold the train for a few moments.

"I want to find the men who caused all the trouble," he said.

The conductor nodded. Raising his voice, he announced:

"There will be a three-minute stop. All passengers for this train please remain on the platform."

The Hardys and Chet hurriedly queried the persons on the platform whether anyone had seen the two men responsible for pushing the brothers onto the track. But none of the crowd had noticed anyone running away from the scene. They had been looking toward the street to see who had screamed. The train whistle blew.

"I guess it's no use," Frank declared. "Those guys have probably skipped out."

When the three boys were seated in the train, Chet remarked, "Do you think the person who screamed had anything to do with the job?"

"Yes," Frank answered. "The whole setup was planned."

"The writer of that note meant business!" Joe exclaimed.

"What note?" Chet inquired. When he learned of the warning, he whistled and asked, "Who do you figure signed himself R?"

The Hardys shrugged, saying the initial most likely stood for Ramapan, but might have been borrowed by someone not connected with the tribe.

"Hm," said Chet, cupping his face in his hands, "we may be running right into danger. Maybe—"

"You don't mean you want to go back and not look for the treasure!" Joe exclaimed in mock disgust.

"Well, not exactly, but you fellows have a habit of getting me in tight places."

"Now that we know what we're up against," Frank said grimly, "those platform pushers will have their hands full if they try to pull any more funny business."

"Let's forget about the mystery for a while and enjoy this trip," Chet interposed half an hour later.

"Okay," Joe replied. "I'll switch on the radio."

He snapped open the small portable set he was carrying and adjusted the dials to a program of hit tunes.

"Pretty nice," Chet remarked comfortably.

He brought out a bag of cookies he had thoughtfully provided and passed them around. As they sat watching the countryside speed by, they listened idly to various programs. At last a newscast came on.

Suddenly Frank sat bolt upright. "Listen to that!" he exclaimed.

The announcer's voice came clearly.

"—serious case of sabotage in Chicago. An important government project has been bombed by saboteurs, leaving the place in ruins.

"Fenton Hardy, the famous investigator, is on the scene at this very moment. When interviewed at the scene of the sabotage Mr. Hardy said that he is following up scattered clues, but that so far none of the culprits has been captured. And now for news on the international front—"

Frank clicked the set off. "The gang has struck again!" he exclaimed.

Chet's face wore a puzzled look. "I thought your dad was supposed to be in California. Now he turns up in Chicago."

"That is strange," Joe agreed, frowning. "He must have flown there in a big hurry."

"But I'm sure Mother just heard from him in California." Frank insisted. "As soon as the train arrives, we're supposed to call home, anyway. We'll ask Mother about it."

The train was now moving along more slowly, ascending the rugged mountainous country where the Ramapan community was located. Stone cliffs were evident, forests more prevalent. At last the big Diesel pulled into Lantern Junction.

The Hardys were the first to alight and hurried

to a telephone booth in the station. Joe put in a long-distance call to Bayport.

"Circuits busy," came the reply.

Joe hung up. Two minutes later he tried again.

"Still busy. I'll call you."

The brothers sat down to wait. Chet had ambled in. He saw a candy vending machine and emptied it of chocolates.

"How about looking for a hotel for us?" Frank suggested, and Chet left the station.

Fifteen minutes later the phone rang and Joe leaped to answer it. "I have your party, sir. Deposit the proper coins, please." There was the usual metallic click, then Mrs. Hardy's voice.

"Hello, Mother," Joe said. "We're here." He decided not to mention the episode at the Bayport station. "Mother, have you heard from Dad since we left?"

"Yes."

"We heard a report on the radio," Joe went on, "that he's working on a sabotage case in Chicago. Is that right?"

As she was replying, Frank crowded into the booth with Joe. He could hear her answer plainly.

"I heard the report too. I'm baffled by the whole thing. Your father can't be in two places at once, and I just had a wire from him. It was sent from California!"

Chet came back and sidled up to the boys. "We

can stay at the Grand Hotel," he reported. Joe passed the news along to his mother, then said, "I guess there's nothing we can do about Dad. But keep us posted if you hear of any new developments."

"I will, and take care of yourselves."

"We will. 'Bye now."

Despite the fact that Mrs. Hardy did not seem concerned about her husband, Frank was uneasy. The newscast said that he was in Chicago; but a telegram placed the famous detective in California!

"Let's call his hotel in San Francisco," he suggested. "That will clear up this whole business."

"Okay, but let's register at the Grand first."

As soon as they were in their room Frank gave the operator the call. When the connection was made, he said:

"I'd like to speak to Mr. Fenton Hardy."

"One moment, please," the operator at the hotel replied.

Then a man's voice broke in. "Who is it you want?" he asked.

"Is Mr. Fenton Hardy there?" Frank repeated, leaning close to the receiver. "This is his son, Frank Hardy."

"I can't tell you!" the man replied and hung up.

Frank replaced the receiver, frowning thoughtfully.

" 'Can't tell you,' " he echoed slowly, after telling Joe and Chet the strange reply.

"What did the man mean?" Chet asked, puzzled.

"I'd say the hotel actually doesn't know where Dad is," Joe answered.

"Or it could be that they're obeying instructions from Dad not to tell where he is," Frank reflected. "All of which tells us nothing."

The boys began unpacking in their neat but simply furnished quarters. Frank and Joe would bunk together, with Chet in the adjoining room.

"Boy, wouldn't I give anything to go hunting or fishing up here," Chet remarked. "But we have to find the treasure first."

"Not *we*," Joe corrected. "Frank and I came up here to follow up the key-case clue."

"Have it your way."

The three boys put on warm, sturdy attire for their hike through the woods to the Ramapan village. When they were ready, they went downstairs and asked directions of the clerk how to get to the Ramapan reservation. They were told that the trail through thick woods to the isolated community, which lay miles from any habitation, was a rough one. The clerk strongly advised them not to attempt it until morning.

"No telling what you might meet up with in the dark," he said. "It's bad enough in the daylight."

The man's words were not exaggerated, as the boys learned next morning. The trail to the Ramapans was narrow and twisting, making it necessary for them to walk along Indian file among the tall trees through which the sun slanted down.

Occasionally the stillness of the forest was broken by the cry of an animal or the fluttering of a startled bird. Once the boys jumped back as two deer leaped across their path, and again when they accidentally flushed a pair of woodcock from their resting place.

"Ouch!" Chet cried, as a branch Joe had moved aside slapped against his face.

"What we need now," declared Frank, pulling aside another limb, "is a machete."

"Sure," said Chet. "This is as bad as a jungle."

A moment later the boys found themselves in a small clearing. Pausing to catch their breath which made white clouds in the crisp air, they heard a crackling in the underbrush in the woods beyond.

Suddenly the branches on the other side of the clearing parted and an Indian stepped out to face them! No one spoke.

The man was wearing suede pants and coat with fringes. Long, shiny black hair hung down over his shoulders.

The Indian broke the silence. "No be afraid. I your friend," he addressed them in a strange accent.

"You're a Ramapan?" Frank asked him.

The stranger did not answer the question. Instead, he said:

"I give warning. You, paleface boys. You walk to bad country."

"What do you mean?" Joe demanded.

"You come to unfriendly tribe," the stranger went on. "Very dangerous people."

"Dangerous, eh?" Frank said skeptically. "What's so dangerous about an Indian tribe? These days they're just as peaceful as everyone else."

"You listen to warning, paleface," the man continued, anger in his tones. "Tribe guard deep secret. No want visitors. Chief be angry when he know strangers here."

"Well, thank you," Frank responded, "but I guess we'll take our chances with the tribe."

"You bet," added Joe. "We don't scare easy."

"All right, you find out!" the man cried out threateningly. "I run warn chief. He fix you good! You never get out of forest then."

With that the man turned on his heel and disappeared among the trees. The boys looked at each other dumfounded.

Chet paled. "S-a-a-a-y, fellows," he said shakily, "he sure wasn't fooling—he means business! Maybe we'd better take his advice and turn back."

He looked around warily, as if half expecting a dozen Indian warriors to swoop down on him.

"Not on your life," Joe replied determinedly.

Frank agreed, adding, "I'll bet that fellow isn't even a member of the tribe. That accent he had was too thick. No real Indian talks like that these days. I'm sure he's a phony."

"You mean he faked everything—the Indian rig and the accent?" Chet demanded.

"Sure."

"Then who is he?" Chet asked.

"One of the gang we're trying to track down."

"Up here?" Chet squeaked. "Oh, no!"

"You're right, Frank!" Joe exclaimed. "Quick! Before he gets away, let's follow him!"

CHAPTER XIII

Tom-toms

THE BOYS crashed through the thick brush in hot pursuit of the strange Indian.

"Where'd he go?" Chet puffed.

"Here are fresh footprints!" Frank exclaimed. "Come on!"

They raced along, following the tracks Frank had observed. The narrow, rocky path wound deeper into the dim, silent forest. The trees, towering above them, formed a thick wall on either side of the trail.

"This sure is rugged country," Joe remarked as he turned his ankle on a stone. Rubbing his leg vigorously, he added, "I'd like to know where that fake Indian vamoosed to!"

The young detective got down and put his ear to the ground, but he heard no sound of running footsteps.

The trail suddenly twisted sharply to the right.

Frank, still in the lead, held up his hand, signaling a halt. He began to search the ground carefully.

"The footprints seem to come to an end here," he reported. "We've lost him!"

The boys stood still, looking intently for any indication of which way the man had gone. They came to the conclusion that he had jumped from stone to stone, losing his pursuers completely.

"Well, I guess there's no use searching any more," Frank decided. "We may as well continue on to the Ramapan village after we have a snack." The boys quickly ate sandwiches they had brought along and drank from a sparkling mountain spring.

"Do you think that fellow went to warn the Ramapans?" Chet asked as they set off again. "Maybe we ought to go back and write the chief before we call."

"Sure." Joe grinned. "That's exactly what your great-grandfather would have done."

Chet subsided and plodded on after the other boys. But his face had barely resumed its usual placidity when he cried out tensely:

"Listen!"

The Hardys paused. The sound that came to them was a muffled, regular beat.

"Tom-toms!" Frank exclaimed.

Chet turned pale as the beats grew stronger and more insistent. He scrunched up his shoulders and looked nervously about him:

"S-s-sa-ay, fe-l-l-ows, those tom-toms—maybe that

man we just met was right. What if those Indians are getting ready to attack us!"

Frank and Joe broke into laughter.

"Think you're in cannibal land, eh, Chet," Joe needled, "and the cannibals are going to make stew of you? Well, you might be good eating at that."

"Aw, listen, fellows, I—"

"Aren't you young Chief Wallapatookunk?" Frank added. "We expect you to protect us."

Chet blushed furiously. "Come on," he said with a sudden show of bravery. "Let's push on."

They moved along another quarter of a mile without further disturbance. Then a fawn loped swiftly across their path as if in frightened flight. As it disappeared, the reason became evident. An Indian boy about their own age came out of the woods. He stopped short upon seeing them.

The boy was dressed in clothes similar to their own, but because of his coppery skin and straight black hair one could tell that he was an Indian.

"Hello," he said pleasantly. "What are you fellows doing so deep in the woods? Get lost?"

None of the boys answered at once, for each had noticed the moccasins the boy was wearing. On the toe sections of both appeared the mysterious R, outlined with multicolored beads.

"No, we're not lost," Frank replied finally. "We're heading for the Ramapan village."

The Indian noticed the boys' eyes riveted on his

moccasins. "What's the matter? Something wrong?" he asked with a puzzled air.

Joe answered. "Where did you get those moccasins?" he questioned excitedly.

"Why, right here," replied the boy. "We Ramapans make them."

"Are you a Ramapan?" Frank asked.

"Sure."

Joe seized the Indian's hand joyfully. "Boy, are we glad to see you! We've been trying for days to find out who makes those moccasins!"

"Well, follow me, then," the boy said, smiling. "I can show you plenty more like these. By the way, I'm Ted Whitestone," he said. "My father is Chief Oscar Whitestone of the Ramapans."

The Hardys and Chet introduced themselves. Then Ted turned in the direction of the Indian village. The boys liked his frank and open manner.

"Quite a difference between Ted and that man we met on the trail," Joe whispered to his brother as the quartet moved closer to the Indian community. "Let's ask Ted if he knows him."

Before he had a chance, Chet began asking questions about the tribe.

"No, we don't live in wigwams," the Indian boy replied with a smile. "Just regular houses like everybody else. And we don't dress up in feathers and big war bonnets, either. I hope I'm not disillusioning you fellows," he added with a grin.

"But we heard a tom-tom," said Chet.

"One of the men was practicing for our ceremonial dance that we always celebrate this time of year," Ted explained.

"Say, maybe we saw one of 'em dressed up," Chet suggested.

"I don't think so."

"We met an Indian all dressed up in fringed leather just a few minutes before we met you," Chet told him. "He had a peculiar accent."

Ted's eyes widened in surprise. "That's funny. I can't imagine who it might be. Nobody in our tribe dresses like that or talks with an accent, except old Long Heart, and he's all right. What did the man want?"

Frank told him of the stranger's warning about the cruelty of the Ramapans and how they would resent the boys' presence because the tribe was guarding a secret.

Ted looked concerned. He plucked a branch from a tree thoughtfully. "That's crazy," he declared finally. "Anybody can visit the Ramapan village. But I can't understand why a stranger would want to keep you from coming here. I'm going to tell my father about this as soon as we arrive."

The boys glanced at one another. Were they bringing trouble to the Ramapans or were they running into some? To himself each one thought:

"I'd better watch my step."

"Here we are," Ted announced, as the path suddenly widened and opened into a spacious cleared area.

In front of the boys stretched the Ramapan village, which consisted of a main street with stores and several side roads with small, neat houses, most of them painted white. Off to one side stood a long, low building with many windows in it, and in the other direction was a large field which Ted said was used for athletics and tribal conferences.

As the boys walked along they glanced admiringly around them. Young children were playing in yards, older ones were in a school, and housewives were hanging out clothes or marketing—all in the center of a vast forest.

"This is my home," Ted said to the trio, stopping before a small white house with green shutters.

He led the way inside. A tall, distinguished-looking man, whom the youth resembled, met them at the door.

"Dad," Ted addressed him, "I'd like you to meet Frank and Joe Hardy and Chet Morton."

The boys and Chief Oscar Whitestone shook hands, then smiling warmly, the man added, "Come in, boys. You've had a long hike. We don't often see strangers this deep in the forest."

When Frank told briefly why they had come to the isolated community, Chief Whitestone was very much interested.

"We'll show you the factory where we make our leather products," he offered.

The boys followed Chief Whitestone and his son outside. As the group walked toward the factory, the villagers gave cheery greetings to the head of their tribe. Reaching the long, low building which the boys had noticed before, the chief led the way inside.

"Here's where we do our handicraft work," Ted spoke up proudly, his arm encompassing the long room with a single broad sweep.

As they walked down one of the aisles, his father explained the various kinds of work the craftsmen were doing. "This man is making moccasins," he said.

The visitors peered over the shoulder of an old Indian who was carefully molding strips of leather over a wooden block. The boys could see the outlines of the footwear taking shape. They walked on.

"This man's embossing leather," the chief informed them.

The Indian smiled and went on with his painstaking job of pressing a design onto a square of leather with a heated tool. When he finished, a beautiful cluster of stars appeared.

"Those workers over there are sewing key cases," Chief Whitestone pointed out. The visitors watched as one of them punched a hole in the leather with an awl and expertly drew the thread through.

Frank produced the key case their mother had bought from Breck. "Ever see this before?" he asked Chief Whitestone.

The Indian examined the leather article carefully. "Certainly. It was made right here," he answered. He was about to hand it back when he took another look inside. "Just as I thought, Ted. This is made of that special leather we had. It was in that suitcase full of our work that was stolen a few weeks ago." Turning to Frank, he added, "Where did you come across this?"

The boy explained that they were amateur detectives and related the events of the past few days concerning Breck, who had sold the key case to Mrs. Hardy, Kamp his lawyer, and the man in the blue sweater who had tried to gain access to Mr. Hardy's secret file cabinet.

"If the suitcase was stolen, I suppose you have no idea who took the key cases, Chief Whitestone?" Joe said, unable to hide his disappointment.

"I'm afraid I haven't," the man replied. "You see," he explained, "all our work is carried out of here in suitcases, since we can't get a truck or car through the trail. Then it's taken by train to Williamsville where it's turned over to a distributor. He markets everything for us."

The boys listened carefully as the chief went on, "A couple of weeks ago our messenger left the suitcase unguarded in the railroad station, and when he came back to get the bag, it was gone. That's all we know about it."

"I'd say we ought to leave here at once and track down Breck," said Frank, "if it weren't for that strange man we met in the woods. He's connected with this mystery I'm sure. I think we'll stay around Lantern Junction for a few days and track him down."

"I wish you luck," Chief Whitestone said.

He started forward again. When the tour ended and they were outside, he turned to face Frank and Joe.

"So you're detectives," he remarked. "And you're staying around here for a while."

"That's right," Frank replied, wondering what the chief was leading up to.

Smiling at them, he said, "How would you boys like to solve a mystery for me—an old mystery of the Ramapans."

CHAPTER XIV

A Jeweled Dagger

ANOTHER mystery to solve! This one with an Indian background. The Hardys' eyes gave Chief Whitestone an affirmative answer. Nevertheless, Frank said aloud:

"We'll do our best, Chief Whitestone."

"And when he tells you that," Chet spoke up, "it means they'll solve it."

Ted and his father smiled as the brothers blushed at the compliment.

"When can we start?" Joe asked. "We'd like to begin right now because we're due back at school in a week or so."

"Yes, and solving it depends a little on where we'll have to go," Frank added. "Is it far away?"

"The answer is that you can begin work right here as soon as I tell you the story," the chief replied. "In fact, you'll have to solve the mystery in the next few

111

days or else you will have to wait for a whole year."

With this mysterious introduction he invited the boys to go back to his home and hear the full story. Seated before an open fire in a cozy room filled with Indian relics, he began the strange tale.

"We Ramapans are an old tribe. Like most Indian tribes nowadays we were once a great and powerful nation, a leader among the Indians in this part of the country.

"But as the years passed, and the white men spread out, our territories grew smaller. Our people became fewer in number as tribal warfare and sickness took their toll. Gradually, the Ramapans' power was so weakened that we were forced to move north. This was many generations ago.

"Then, gradually," the chief continued, "the wars stopped, and modern medicine cut down our death rate. We became prosperous, but still we were small and missed our former greatness," he said with a faraway look in his eyes.

"The tribe carefully held on to its savings from fishing and trapping. Then fifty-nine years ago the leaders made a decision. With my father as chief, they decided to pool their resources and move down from the wild north country. The place they chose was this very acreage, which was the site where our ancestors had lived."

The boys had scarcely moved as the fascinating tale unfolded.

"My father and the tribe bought this forest and the cleared land from the estate of a man named York."

York! The name of one of the suspected gang!

"Was his name Philip York?" Frank asked.

"No," Chief Whitestone replied. "It was Amos York. But after the tribe set up their new home, they didn't find the peace and security they had expected."

"What happened?" Joe asked. The chief had paused to strike a match to his long pipe.

He puffed a few times, then continued. "A neighboring tribe started to raid and rob the Ramapans almost as soon as they had settled here. They came every night, stealing and wrecking and striking terror into our people's hearts. But the Ramapans fought back even against heavy odds," the chief said proudly.

"My father, who was old and weak, was fearful the enemy would steal our deed to the property, as well as other valuable papers and tribal records. So he buried them secretly, together with a jeweled dagger worth thousands of dollars that the Ramapans had had in their possession for generations. They had confiscated it after a battle with a French army two hundred years previously."

"Where did your father bury the papers and the dagger?" Frank asked him.

Chief Whitestone shook his head. "That's the mystery. Not long after my father buried them, he became ill and finally we realized he was dying.

"According to the laws of our tribe, I would become chief of the Ramapans. Everyone knew my father had buried the papers and the dagger, but the place was a secret. So I asked him where they were. At first he was too weak to reply.

" 'Father, Chief of the Ramapans,' I said pleadingly, 'tell me, your son, the next chief, where the papers are buried.'

"My father was sinking rapidly, but he opened his eyes with great will power and whispered: 'My son—my son—papers—dagger—buried where a crisscross shadow is cast in the light of the Hunter's Moon.' "

As the chief stopped speaking, there was complete silence for several seconds, then the Hardys looked at Chet. His face wore a smug look, as if to say: "You fellows wouldn't believe me! There is a treasure buried in a crisscross shadow!"

Chief Whitestone continued after a moment. "That was the only clue my father gave and I've never been able to find the place."

"It doesn't sound like an easy problem," Frank remarked.

"That's not all," Chief Whitestone interrupted. "Not long ago two strangers appeared in the village. When I asked them what they wanted, they said they wished to buy our land and were prepared to offer a fair price for it.

" 'No,' I told them, 'we wouldn't sell for all the

money in the world. This is our home. The tribe has grown and prospered here after many generations of hardship. Our land is not for sale.' "

"But that didn't end it," Ted took up the story. "The men were insistent. Finally, one of them got mad and started to yell. 'Look, Chief,' he said to my father, 'I'm warning you! You'd better sell to us if you know what's good for you.' "

"That's right." Chief Whitestone nodded. " 'What do you mean?' I asked them.

" 'Just this,' the man replied. 'This land isn't yours. You Ramapans don't have a clear title to it.'

"I laughed at that, but he said, 'You think it's funny, eh? Well, we can prove you haven't got a clear title!' Then they stomped out of the house and disappeared.

"I'm afraid those men will find the deed before we do and steal it," Chief Whitestone said. "Unfortunately, we have no other proof of ownership. The courthouse where our deed was recorded burned a few years ago and the papers were lost."

"Then those men can make it very hard for you," Joe said.

"Yes. After the fire, ads were run in the papers for people to bring in their deeds and have them recorded again, but we couldn't do that, of course."

"So it was easy for those men to find out your deed is missing," Frank surmised. "Well, we'll certainly try to find it for you."

"Haven't you any protection?" Chet interposed.

"Maybe," the chief said. "After sixty years of possession, the tribe will own the land automatically—even without a deed. It's a state law. But we have several months to go before the time is up. Until then, we're at the mercy of anyone who finds those papers!"

"You're pretty sure that they haven't been found already?" Ted questioned his father.

"We can't be certain someone hasn't taken them, of course," the chief answered.

"I doubt it," Frank commented. "If they had, you would have heard about it by this time. Either the papers would have been returned by honest people or you would have had trouble before this with real thieves."

"How about those men who were here?" Chief Whitestone asked.

"I don't think that they would have offered to buy the land if they could have got it free."

"But I'll bet they're looking for the deed," Joe remarked. "So it's going to be a race. Come on, fellows. Let's get started!"

"I like your enthusiasm." The chief smiled. "But first I suggest we have something to eat. And later, why don't you move in here so you can be handy to your work?"

"Thank you," Frank replied. "We'll do that. And along with solving your mystery, we'll do some sleuthing on our own case."

By the time they had finished a meal of roast deer, corn bread, and fried apples prepared by Mrs. Whitestone, it had grown dark.

"You'd better put up with us tonight," Ted suggested. "Then you can go back and get your things at the hotel tomorrow."

Chet stretched and yawned. "I'm ready for the sack," he said as the Hardys grinned.

Since they could do no more sleuthing at this hour, the boys accepted Ted's hospitality and slept on cots in his room.

After breakfast next morning, Ted said, "The Indian boys are having a lacrosse game. How would you like to watch it for a while?"

"We sure would," Joe said enthusiastically.

As the Hardys and Chet stood watching on the side lines, they talked over what they had read about the game. Lacrosse was an old Indian game, they recalled, played with a hard rubber ball which is carried or thrown with a long-handled racket. Years ago, Indian tribes often played each other in long and bloody contests with a hundred men on each side.

Even the modern game which Ted was playing, with ten men on a side, was a wonderful athletic conditioner. Frank, Joe, and Chet watched admiringly as Ted, playing center, stepped into the circle at mid-field and faced the ball with his opponent.

At the referee's signal Ted's lightning-like crosse

scooped up the white ball. He cleared it to a teammate and the battle was on.

"What speed!" Joe exclaimed as the Indians raced and twisted down the field.

Ted had the ball again, but a hard body block knocked it from his stick. An enemy player was on it like a hungry kingfisher after a minnow.

The ball whipped back and forth with the players on the run. When it was flung at the net, Ted's goalee blocked it off his chest.

As the pellet caromed away, the chief's son scooped it up and hurled the ball one hundred yards down field where an attack man was waiting.

"What a tricky maneuver!" Chet exclaimed.

Ted's teammate dodged a defense man, closed in on the goal, and drilled the ball into the corner of the net for a score.

"Real team play!" Frank remarked.

"They'd make swell football players for Bayport High," Chet remarked, thinking of the tough games that lay ahead. "They're natural athletes."

As the lacrosse contest continued, Frank nudged Joe. "We'd better be getting on our sleuthing job."

Joe nodded in agreement. Leaving Chet to watch the rest of the game, they walked away to map out a plan of action.

"First thing we'll have to do is move our belongings in from town," Joe suggested.

"Right you are," Frank agreed. "But there's no

need for all of us to go back. I'll take care of that little matter. I'll put all we need in one bag and check the others."

"I'll start hunting around here for clues," Joe declared.

The brothers walked to the edge of the settlement, then Frank went down the trail that led to town. Joe ambled along the street until he reached the leather-crafts building. Nonchalantly he walked around it, to observe the layout of the structure.

"Guess I'll go inside," Joe told himself. "Maybe if I talk with some of the workers—"

The sound of a door opening interrupted his thoughts. The boy stood motionless as he saw one of the craftsmen emerge from the rear entrance. Joe ducked behind a tree and watched as the man looked intently in every direction.

"He acts as though he doesn't want to be seen," Joe thought.

Abruptly the man turned and set out briskly through the forest. Joe lost no time in following, and trailed him noiselessly, keeping out of sight.

Suddenly the Indian stopped and Joe concealed himself behind an evergreen. The man began stripping bark from a tree, all the while whistling in a carefree manner.

Joe, puzzled, arose slowly from his hiding place. "If that's all that guy came here for," he mused, "why did he act so leery of being seen?"

The next moment the Indian lighted a cigarette. After a few puffs he stamped it out and started back for the crafts building.

Joe grinned as he recalled a *No Smoking* sign in the building.

"So he just slipped out to have a smoke. He sure had me fooled."

Joe started walking back toward the village. Suddenly he stopped in his tracks. What was that strange scraping noise behind him off to his right?

He stealthily retraced his steps in the direction of the sound, which led him to a small clearing. Joe barely restrained an exclamation when he saw a man digging in the hard-packed earth.

It was the stranger in the suede-fringed suit whom the boys had met in the forest the day before!

Without hesitation, Joe approached the digger.

"This time I'll find out what his game is," the youth was thinking when a twig snapped behind him.

Joe looked over his shoulder in time to see a man leaping toward him, brandishing a lacrosse stick.

He tried to duck, but it was too late. With a violent blow, the man brought the stick smashing down on the boy's head.

Without uttering a cry, Joe crumpled to the earth!

CHAPTER XV

A Puzzling Telegram

A QUARTER of an hour passed before Joe stirred. Opening his eyes, he was conscious only of a severe pain in the top of his head. Feeling the damp earth against his cheek, the young detective realized he was lying on the ground.

"What happened to me?" he asked himself dully.

With what seemed like a superhuman effort, Joe lifted himself on one elbow and saw the trees about him. Only then did he remember what had occurred.

"—going toward the man in the fringed suede suit when I turned around and saw someone behind me —had a lacrosse stick in his hand—" Joe put his hand to his head and felt a large bump where the blow had fallen.

"I'd better get back to the Ramapan village," he muttered. "Got to warn Chief Whitestone about those men."

Joe staggered to his feet. Leaning against a tree to keep from falling, he waited a long minute to get his bearings.

"Easy does it," he told himself.

His head throbbed. Swaying from side to side, Joe took a few uncertain steps. It was hard going but finally he reached the edge of the village. Only a few yards ahead he could get help.

But he had to sit down and rest for several minutes before proceeding. Suddenly he saw a familiar figure hurrying up the street.

"Chet!" he tried to call, but his words were barely audible and his friend headed up the street out of sight. He started for the Whitestone house, stopping frequently to rest for a moment.

"Another few yards and I'll be there at last," he told himself.

Suddenly he heard a cry behind him. "Joe, Joe, what happened?" A friendly hand reached out to support him.

"Ted! Oh, gosh, I'm glad to see you."

"Who hit you?" Ted exclaimed, seeing a huge, bloody lump on the top of Joe's head.

"Don't know," he gasped as the Indian boy steered him toward his house.

As they reached the steps, Chief Whitestone came out, his face showing his concern. He helped Ted lift Joe and soon the injured youth was resting on a couch.

Ted hurried for the village doctor. After a searching examination the physician concluded that there was no skull fracture but told Joe that he might have a headache for a few hours and to call him if anything else developed. He dressed the wound and left.

A sigh escaped Ted's lips. "Thought you were a goner when I saw you staggering down that street, Joe," he said, and smiled in relief.

But Chief Whitestone was not smiling. He was red with anger.

"That fellow tried to kill you!" he exclaimed. He clenched his pipe, the knuckles showing white against the dark bowl.

"Ted," he went on, "I'm very much concerned about this business. I want you to make inquiries around the village while Joe takes it easy."

"Don't worry about me, Chief Whitestone," Joe insisted. "We detectives are used to some roughing up now and then."

"Did you get a good look at the man who hit you?" Ted wanted to know.

Joe stared down at the white rug that covered the floor. "I saw him," he admitted. "But he was somebody I'd never seen before. I couldn't identify him," he said ruefully. "All I remember is that lacrosse stick coming down—lacrosse stick—lacros—" Joe repeated. "That's it! The lacrosse stick may have come from your supply of them!" he exclaimed, half rising from the couch.

Ted grasped his arm excitedly. "Hold on a minute. I'll dash over there and see if one is missing. I know how many we had."

In a few moments Ted returned, a grim expression on his face.

"You were right, Joe," he cried. "There's a lacrosse stick missing!"

Joe thought for a moment. "It couldn't have been one of the players. I'd have recognized him. That leaves only one possibility—"

"You mean someone stole the stick?"

"That's right, Ted."

At this moment Chet hurried in, having heard from a child that the doctor had been calling on "the sick white boy."

"Joe!" he exclaimed, pale with fright. "What happened?"

While Chet was listening to Joe's story, Frank Hardy, unaware of what had befallen his brother, strode briskly down the forest trail and finally reached Lantern Junction. He went at once to the Grand Hotel.

"We're moving out," he told the pleasant clerk.

"Going home so soon?"

"No. We're going to try the woods." Frank leaned over confidentially. "As a matter of fact, we're staying with the Ramapans, and if you don't mind, when any messages come here, we'll pay to have them delivered up there in care of the chief."

"Glad to oblige you," the clerk said.

After paying the bill, packing, and arranging for all the bags but one to be checked at the hotel, Frank decided to telephone his mother and find out if the mix-up concerning Mr. Hardy's reported presence had been straightened out.

Frank entered the phone booth in the lobby. While waiting for the operator to complete the long-distance call to Bayport, he pondered the mystery of his father's appearance in Chicago and the West Coast at the same time.

After several moments the operator told him the call was ready and he heard his mother's voice.

"Frank? What a relief to hear from you!"

"Anything wrong?" he wanted to know, detecting a note of agitation in her voice.

"Yes," she hurried on. "I was afraid those men might have been after you and Joe again. They've been here."

"What do you mean, Mother?"

"There's been another attempted burglary in our house!"

Frank grabbed at the mouthpiece. "Are you and Aunt Gertrude all right? Did you see the burglar? Did he get anything?"

"We're all right," Mrs. Hardy replied quickly. "But the burglar got away. I can't tell you whether he stole anything or not. Chief Collig is working on the case right now."

As Frank was about to express his pleasure that the canny police officer was on the job, his mother went on, "There's more news of your father."

"Is it good news?"

"Well, I don't know. Another case of sabotage," Mrs. Hardy told him. "This time in St. Louis."

"St. Louis! That gang's getting bolder all the time!"

"A laboratory was swept by flames last night and the reports of secret experiments which scientists were working on went up in smoke," his mother continued. "Your father was reported on the scene."

"Good!" Frank exclaimed. "At least the investigation's in capable hands."

"But I'm worried, Son. I tried to get in touch with your father in St. Louis through the police, but the authorities there told me he had disappeared."

"Disappeared!" Frank repeated anxiously, then said, "Maybe he's only gone underground to track down the gang."

"I don't know what to think, Frank," Mrs. Hardy replied. "Just a little while ago I got a message that makes everything completely baffling."

"Message from Dad?"

"Yes. And it came from California! All the telegram said was 'Detained in California. Will wire again.'"

"But the report of the sabotage placed Dad in St. Louis."

"Exactly." Mrs. Hardy sighed. "I think the wire from California is a hoax!"

"Something's fishy, that's sure," Frank agreed. "But don't worry. I have a couple of ideas on how to get to the bottom of this, Mother. I'll let you know when I learn something."

"All right, dear, and give my love to Joe."

Frank left the booth and eased himself onto one of the big leather couches in the lobby. Rubbing his jaw as he sat lost in thought, Frank toyed with several plans of going about learning the truth of his father's whereabouts. Finally he snapped his fingers.

"I have it!" he told himself excitedly.

Rushing back to the phone booth, he asked the operator to connect him with John Bryant, detective, in San Francisco. The man was a friend of Fenton Hardy and his sons and could be depended upon to help the family.

"Hello, Mr. Bryant," he said, after the connection was made. "This is Frank Hardy of Bayport."

"Hello, Frank. Glad to hear from you. Great things your father's doing these days."

"That's why I'm calling. We're worried about reports that he's in two places at once."

Mr. Bryant chuckled. "I didn't know even a Hardy could do that."

Frank quickly explained the mystery of his father's seemingly double appearances, both times where sabotage was involved.

"This is my plan," he said, speaking guardedly. "Will you check on Dad at his hotel, and then wire the result to Sam Radley at the Bayport Hospital? It's important that you send the message to Sam. One to us probably would be intercepted or tampered with. Mother's been getting some, but she thinks they may be phonies."

"I'll be glad to," Mr. Bryant promised. "Don't blame you for being worried."

Assuring Frank of his fullest co-operation, he said good-by. As the boy left the booth, he looked carefully around the room to see if any suspicious characters were lurking about. Finding the lobby empty except for the desk clerk, he hurried to a writing desk.

"I'd better warn Sam Radley to expect a message from Mr. Bryant," he thought, picking up a pen.

After writing a few lines to his father's injured associate about his plan, Frank wished him a speedy recovery and signed his name. Folding the paper, he inserted it in an envelope which he addressed in plain block letters to disguise his handwriting. He sealed the envelope, stamped it, and deposited the letter in a mailbox at the end of the lobby.

"Nobody will dare tamper with Uncle Sam's mails," he told himself in satisfaction.

Waving to the desk clerk, Frank walked out of the hotel, the suitcase of clothes for the three boys in his hand.

As he turned down the street that led to the Rama-pan trail, Frank saw a familiar figure hurrying toward him.

"Why, it's Chet!" Frank said to himself. "What could be up? He looks worried."

Chet raced toward him, waving his arms in great agitation. He was red in the face and puffing from the long run.

"Frank! Frank!" he was calling excitedly.

CHAPTER XVI

The Hunter's Moon

FRANK hurried to meet Chet, who was gasping for breath from his exertions.

"Ran most of the way," he panted, "to tell you about—about Joe."

"Joe? Is he in trouble?" Frank clutched Chet in anxiety.

"Attacked by stranger—knocked out!" Chet heaved as he tried to regain his wind.

"Knocked out! By whom? Tell me!" Frank shook Chet in his excitement.

Sitting down on the curb, and pausing frequently to get his breath, Chet recounted Joe's experience in the woods.

"The doctor's seen him. Thinks he'll be okay."

"*Thinks?* Doesn't he know?" Frank pleaded for more information.

"Hold on!" Chet begged. "I'm sure Joe'll be all right. What I came to town for was the police."

"Go on," Frank urged.

Chet arose, his breathing restored. "Ted and I went to find Joe's attacker," he said.

"Any luck?" Frank asked. He was seething at the thought of his brother's being brutally set upon.

"We located the spot where the man attacked Joe," Chet replied, "and searched around. Finally we saw tracks leading to the main trail and followed them for a few yards until they were lost."

"Did you find any other clue?" Frank questioned him, disappointed that they had not caught Joe's assailant.

Chet grinned in satisfaction. "We found this."

Digging inside his jacket, he produced a package wrapped in cloth.

"What is it?" Frank asked, puzzled.

Chet unwrapped the cloth. "A piece of the lacrosse stick used on Joe!"

"Good work, Chet!" Frank cried.

Carefully he examined the piece which was the handle section of the stick. One end was splintered, showing that it had been broken by a violent blow.

"You're taking this to the police?" he asked Chet.

"Sure. For fingerprints!"

Frank frowned. "There must be a lot of them. Dozens of players probably have handled this stick."

Chet's face fell. "Gosh," he said, "I didn't think of that."

"As long as you brought the stick you might as

well have it checked. The police station is right around the corner," Frank told him.

The boys went there at once. Frank gave the desk sergeant their names and asked for the chief. The visitors were ushered into his office.

"Frank Hardy, eh?" he greeted them. He was a short, plump man, who gave the boys a warm smile and told them to call him Mike. "Any relation to Fenton Hardy, the famous detective?"

"His son. My brother's at the Ramapan village."

"Well, well," the officer said. "What brings you boys up to this neck of the woods? Some mystery?"

Quickly Frank explained their mission to find a thief named Breck. When he told the officer what had happened to Joe, the police chief looked grave.

"Any clues?" he asked.

Chet produced the lacrosse stick and told about finding it near the spot where Joe had been attacked.

"I thought the fellow's fingerprints might be on it," he added hopefully.

"It won't take long to find out," Mike replied, then carried the piece of wood into a back room.

While he was gone, the boys talked over the various aspects of the mystery, and Frank whispered the latest news about his father.

"Good night!" Chet exclaimed.

A short while later the officer returned, a satisfied look on his face. In one hand he carried a Manila folder.

"Well, Chet," he said, "you hit the jackpot this time. We found a jailbird's fingerprints on this stick!"

A broad grin broke over the boy's features. Frank congratulated him.

"Whose prints are they?" he asked.

Mike opened the folder and took out some papers. "Fellow by the name of Smirkis," he told them. "About forty years old. Small-time crook. Got a year for robbery some months back. He was released a short time ago for good behavior. Lives right here in town."

"Smirkis, eh?" Frank mused. "I wonder if he's connected with the gang we're after."

"I couldn't say. He wasn't too bad a fellow, but he may have met someone in prison who put ideas into his head," Mike said.

"Where does he live?" Frank asked.

"We just checked with the landlady of his rooming house, but she said he hasn't been home in a couple of days. I've sent out an alarm for him.

"We'll need your brother to identify Smirkis as the assailant when we catch up with him. Meanwhile, take care of yourselves," Mike warned.

The boys thanked him, ate a light lunch, and then headed back to the Indian village. Frank was anxious to see Joe and was glad to find him feeling better.

Next day, while Joe was recuperating, he and Frank talked over with Ted and Chet the clue to the missing papers and the jeweled dagger. Chief White-stone had gone to Lantern Junction on business.

"Buried in the crisscross shadow at the time of the Hunter's Moon," Chet mulled over the Indian chief's statement. "Wonder what made the crisscross shadow?"

He and Joe made several suggestions that were immediately discounted by Ted because they did not jibe with the legend.

"The story goes this way. 'And the chief buried the dagger of the many bright eyes and the papers of the paleface writing while at his hunter's dwelling in the early moonrises.' "

"Hunter's dwelling!" Frank cried. "I have it! A hunter's dwelling could be a wigwam. The crisscross shadow was made by wigwam poles!"

"Of course!" exclaimed Ted. "Why didn't we Ramapans think of that?"

Chet looked puzzled.

"The tops of wigwam poles cast a crisscross shadow," Ted went on, "and the Ramapans used wigwams."

"And the Hunter's Moon is in October, isn't it?" Chet asked.

"Yes, it's the full moon of October and it rises early just like the legend says," Ted answered. "In October the angle the moon makes with the earth is very slight, so it rises as the full moon very soon after sunset."

"We're going into the Hunter's Moon right now,"
Frank said. "That's what your father meant, wasn't
it, Ted, when he urged us to solve the mystery and
find the deed soon?"

"Yes."

"First thing to do," Frank said, "is to find out
where the chief's wigwam stood when he buried the
treasure. Have you any idea where that was?" he
asked Ted.

"It was near where the tribe used to hold its cere-
monials," Ted replied. "The records say that the
ceremonial rock was located where a stream, forked
like a serpent's tongue, cuts through the warrior's
place of honor."

"What does that mean?" Chet questioned.

"Long ago, returning warriors were honored for a
whole day by feasting and—"

"Sounds good." The stout boy beamed. "They
probably had roast moose; all they wanted."

"Let's get going," Frank interrupted.

Ted led the way to the area where the old cere-
monials had been held. He said that it had not been
used in his lifetime.

"Then we're going to have a hard job locating the
rock in this overgrown tangle," Joe remarked, looking around.

He had insisted upon going along but the others
made him sit on the side lines and not exert himself.
Disgusted, Joe sat down on a log which had fallen

across what once had been the fork in the stream mentioned in the legend.

"Looks as if we're stumped," he said ten minutes later when the boys found no evidence of a large flat rock.

Meanwhile Frank, who had squatted down near him and was sighting in the direction of the main stream, gave a shout.

"There it is, fellows!"

He ran toward a little mound of silt and moss that they had overlooked in their search. Digging excitedly for a few seconds, and scraping away the incrustation of many years, he exposed a huge, flat rock to the light.

"And now to find out where the chief's wigwam stood," Joe said.

"It's beyond me," Chet commented, and wearily sat down on the rock.

"Paleface boy want to know where old chief wigwam stood?" a voice behind him said.

Chet jumped in surprise and whirled to look at an elderly Indian wearing a leather shirt and leggings.

"Hello, Long Heart," Ted greeted the old man.

The boys had seen him around the village, dressed in the outmoded costume of the Ramapans. Ted introduced him as the oldest member of the tribe.

"He's always telling us boys stories of the old days," Ted said, smiling.

"We do want to know where the old chief's wig-wam stood," Frank said. "Can you help us?"

"My memory not so good—for I am many moons old," Long Heart answered. "But maybe remember where wigwam of great brave stood."

With that, he started walking back and forth, mut-tering to himself. Finally he stopped two hundred feet from the ceremonial rock.

"Here," he said with finality. "Here wigwam of chief. Why paleface want know this?" he asked Ted suspiciously.

After the boy told him the palefaces were trying to find the lost deed in order to save the tribe's land, the old brave's eyes lighted up.

"Me help," he said simply. "You build wigwam with pole fifteen feet long. Me come tonight at rise of moon," and saying no more, he turned his back and went toward the village.

"How do you build a Ramapan wigwam?" Chet asked. "Is it any different from the ones we made at camp?"

"Probably not." Ted grinned. "I guess you pale-faces learned how from us Indians."

Nevertheless, he instructed them as they began their work. They cut down six saplings fifteen feet long and tied them together three feet from the top. Then they raised the poles and spread the legs to form a firm base, pressing them into the ground.

The next step was to lash short, flexible saplings

horizontally across the slanting poles. After that they fastened sections of birch and hemlock bark over them with tough vines and trailing roots. Short poles were used to cover the bark to keep it from curling.

Finally they cut a smoke hole at the top and another for an entrance. The boys stood back proudly to view their work.

"Pretty swell," Chet remarked. "Now if that old moon'll just come out, we'll find that deed for your dad in no time, Ted," he boasted.

"I suppose it's expecting too much to keep this operation a secret from our enemies," Frank remarked. "But let's come here separately tonight and watch for any spies."

"Agreed," they all said.

Just before sunset the Hardys, Chet, Ted, and Chief Whitestone, going by separate routes, arrived at the old ceremonial rock. They found Long Heart waiting impassively for them.

"The weather's holding up," Frank said to his brother. "Only a few clouds."

Slowly the sun sank below the horizon. Then a few minutes later the Hunter's Moon of the legend shone from behind some clouds. Eagerly six pairs of eyes followed the clouds until they blew away.

Suddenly Joe whispered excitedly, "There it is— the crisscross shadow!"

It was true. The poles atop the wigwam made crisscrossed shadows on the moonlit ground.

the hard-packed dirt with renewed vigor. The bright
Hunter's Moon cast an eerie light over the scene,
with stalwart Long Heart standing guard.

Joe, regretful that he was not in condition to help
the others, stationed himself in the shadow of the
wigwam, keeping alert for any intruder—accidental
or planned.

Suddenly he tensed. He strained his ears to catch
a sound over the hard breathing of his friends and
the soft thuds the dirt made as it was shoveled from
the pit. The sound came again.

"A twig being stepped on in the woods," Joe told
himself. "I'd better have a look!"

Quietly he slipped among the trees from which the
mysterious crackling had come and looked around.

C-r-r-a-c-c-k!

Stepping carefully, Joe moved ahead in the direction of the sound. He peered through the maze of
moonlight and shadows. Ahead he thought he could
detect the shadow of a man moving silently among
the trees!

Joe tried to follow the ghostly figure. But it kept
eluding him and finally disappeared. Wondering
who it could have been, Joe retraced his steps to the
clearing where the others still were working indus-
triously.

"Find anything yet?" Joe called out.

Suddenly Chief Whitestone tossed his shovel aside
and clambered out of the hole. The others followed.

"Not a thing!" he replied to Joe.

"We're getting no place here," Frank said. "I guess it's useless to dig any more. There are certainly no buried papers in this spot."

"Looks like you're right," Ted agreed. "I guess we had the wrong spot for the wigwam, or the wrong crisscross shadow."

In the moonlight the disappointment on everyone's face was plain to be seen.

"Buck up, fellows," Joe said encouragingly. "Maybe after a good night's sleep we can figure out where we failed to interpret the clue in the legend correctly."

"Right you are, Joe," the chief said. "Let's return home. We'll all have hot drinks, then go straight to bed."

As the others gathered up their tools, Joe took Frank aside. Swiftly he told him of the incident in the woods, and his suspicions that the group had been spied upon by a prowler while they were digging.

"No use worrying the others about it," he said. "Listen! Let's you and I stay overnight in the wigwam and keep watch for intruders."

"Great idea," Frank agreed. "The wigwam's weather-tight, and we'll bring some blankets."

"I'm with you. We'll tell the others."

They asked Chet if he wanted to stay, but their friend preferred the warm, comfortable bed in the chief's home. He offered to bring the blankets to them, however.

Chief Whitestone and Ted protested strongly when they heard the plan, but the Hardys insisted.

"We said we'd help you solve this mystery," Frank reminded the Indians, "and that's exactly what we intend to do!"

As the others trooped slowly out of the clearing back to the village, Frank glanced at the moon. "Look!" he pointed. "Clouds gathering up there. Bad weather ahead."

"Let's hurry and get things ready for the night," Joe suggested. "We'll need a fire."

Quickly they gathered dead pine limbs and brush and in a short while had a small, cheerful fire blazing inside the wigwam. Chet returned with several blankets, then said good night.

As the boys finished adjusting the bark door, Joe held out his hand. "Snow," he said. "Well, I'll take the first watch. You get some sleep."

In a few moments Frank's regular breathing indicated he was asleep. Bundling warmly, Joe took up his guard duty. The early snow began falling more thickly. After a couple of hours, he woke his brother.

"How's the weather?" Frank asked.

"Snowing pretty hard. Nothing stirring out there. But keep your eyes open," he warned.

During Frank's watch, the snow gradually turned

to fine rain, but by the time he changed watches, it had stopped.

"Starting to turn mighty cold out there," he said as Joe took up his post.

Morning finally came. The temperature was way down, and when the dawn broke, the clearing and the woods were covered with a dazzling glaze of ice.

There was a rustling at the door to the wigwam and Ted poked his head through the opening.

"Good morning, fellows. Anything happen during the night?"

"Not a thing."

Joe's eyes were attracted by a curious stick Ted was carrying. He asked what it was.

"A snow snake," the Indian replied with a smile. "It's for playing an ancient Indian game," he explained, holding up the stick for their inspection.

It was long and highly polished, flat on one side and curved on the other. On the end that turned up was the carved head of a snake.

"How do you play the game?" Frank asked.

"It's easy," Ted answered, laughing.

Grasping the stick in the thumb and fingers of his right hand, while resting the snakehead end on the icy surface of the snow, he sent it skimming across the snow with a long sweeping underhand throw. The snake whizzed over the clearing with amazing speed and buried itself in a melting snowbank.

"Wowee! That's something!" Joe cried.

"Here," Ted said. "You try it."

The Hardys took turns. At first the snake either buried its head in the snow after traveling a short distance or else veered to one side and overturned. But after some practice they finally got the knack of throwing it.

"Look at that!" Ted said, as Frank pitched one that found its mark, then went to retrieve it.

But Joe was not listening. He was staring intently at a man who was emerging stealthily from the underbrush. As the stranger reached the clearing, Joe cried out in startled recognition:

"That's my attacker!"

With a leap, he charged after the man, the others following. The stranger fled into the woods, but as he reached another clearing the boys were still dogging his steps.

"Maybe I can stop him!" Frank thought.

Halting in his tracks, he took careful aim with the snow snake. Then, with a powerful sweep of his arm, the boy sent it whizzing across the icy ground.

Straight to its mark the snake traveled! It hit the mysterious stranger on the foot and tripped him. He fell to the ground.

"Bull's-eye!" Joe cried as the boys raced to capture the man.

In a moment he was their prisoner and stood glowering at them. Ted pinned his hands behind his back.

"You're the man who whacked me with the lacrosse stick! You're Smirkis!" Joe said accusingly.

"All right, I'm Smirkis. But I never whacked any of you," the man protested.

"No?" Joe said skeptically. "Well, your fingerprints were on the lacrosse stick. What's more, I saw you sneaking around while we were digging last night, didn't I?"

"No, I didn't spy on you." Smirkis shook his head vigorously, but he had paled at Joe's mention of the fingerprints.

"You'd better come with us to police headquarters," Frank said.

"Wait a minute!" Smirkis cried out anxiously. "I'll make a deal with you boys."

"A deal? What kind of deal?" Joe asked.

"If you'll let me go, I'll give you some vital information. How about it?" he whined.

The boys looked at one another questioningly. It was attractive bait Smirkis was offering. His vital information might lead to the solution of the mystery!

Joe and Frank moved out of the man's hearing to talk it over. "I don't trust him," Joe whispered.

Frank nodded. "Let's try to trick him into telling us what the information is."

He turned to Smirkis. "I know what you're going to tell us. That the men who want to buy this property hired you to get rid of us!"

"How'd you know that?" Smirkis gasped.

No sooner had he uttered the words than a strange voice behind them cried, "Shut up!"

Frank and Joe wheeled around to face three masked men, poised to attack!

CHAPTER XVIII

A Rough Trip

As THE Hardys leaped at their attackers, one of the masked men side-stepped them to clamp a hand over Ted's mouth as he started to give the Ramapan war cry for help. Locked in a fierce struggle, Joe and Frank hurled their opponents to the ground. The boys fought with every bit of strength they could muster, but outnumbered, the odds were against them.

"Okay, tie 'em up and blindfold 'em," ordered one of the men, who seemed to be the leader.

The young detectives and their Indian friend were tightly bound with ropes and their eyes covered with kerchiefs.

"All set?" the same voice asked. "Let's go! You know the plan, men."

Frank and Joe were roughly grasped by the shoulders and pushed.

"Start walking," the leader ordered.

As they trudged off, the Hardys heard sounds heading in another direction.

"They're separating us from Ted," Joe whispered to Frank.

"Keep quiet!" the leader commanded. "No talking."

They walked in silence. Unfriendly hands grasped them by their jackets whenever they stumbled.

"Ain't so high and mighty now, are you, eh?" one of the men taunted them.

"You won't be so anxious to stick your noses in other people's business when we get through with you," another sneered.

"You can't win, anyway," the leader said. "In a short while the Indians will be gone!"

"You're trying to bluff us," Frank spoke up boldly. "Where are you taking us?"

"Bluffing, you say? Just wait and see. This land's going to change hands, and you can't stop it!"

After a silence of many minutes, one of the men said, "What about Smirkis? He talks too much!"

"The boss'll take care of him after he does that job for us."

So Smirkis was the one who had taken Ted away!

Presently the boys were halted. Then hands lifted them up and lowered them into something narrow that swayed from side to side.

"Okay," the leader said. "Let's shove off."

"A canoe!" Frank realized as they began to move and he heard the regular rhythm of a paddle being dipped into the water.

Though he had been told not to speak, Frank had to know whether Joe was still with the party. He decided to take a chance and called, "Joe!"

"Here!" came the reply, apparently from another canoe.

Immediately the brothers were smacked soundly on their cheeks and told if they made another outcry they would be gagged. However, they felt a temporary sense of relief that they were still together.

After a silent trip of an hour the bottom of the canoe scraped against sand, and in a moment the boys were jerked to their feet and dragged across the ground. Next, they were lifted into a vehicle with its engine running. They started off over a rough road.

Joe and Frank were ravenous, not having eaten for many hours, but the men made no offer of food. The car rumbled on for what seemed like an eternity.

"We must be a long way from the Ramapans by now!" Frank thought. "Where are we going?"

Forty minutes later the car stopped. The brothers were hauled out. The wind was blowing in gusts as if a storm were brewing.

"What next?" the Hardys thought, then heard a plane's motor being tuned up. They were hoisted into it and the plane took off.

By the way it yawed and jounced after they were in the air, Frank and Joe realized that they had been stowed in the tail section.

It was a rough trip, with no chance for them to try loosening their bonds. The plane rose and fell with dizzying speed as it was buffeted through the air. The drumming of hail against the fuselage indicated that the storm was becoming more violent, and the swift changes of pressure on their eardrums were sickening.

"I hope that pilot knows his business," Joe whispered nervously.

"He certainly isn't handling the ship properly for this storm," Frank said as the plane plunged earthward.

"We're in a spin!" Joe cried. "That fool pilot's going to kill us!"

Suddenly the plane was jerked back straight and leveled off! It rocked violently, but the spin had been checked as if by a miracle!

Frank and Joe sighed in relief.

When the plane landed, it bounced a couple of times. Since the boys could not feel the rolling of wheels, they concluded they had landed on water. The door opened and the brothers were gagged. Then they were carried out.

"Okay," the leader ordered curtly after they reached the top of a stairway, "cover your own faces and then take off the boys' blindfolds."

The Hardys blinked as the light, though dim, struck their eyes. Peering around, they found themselves in a gloomy, shabbily furnished room with one small light. Their masked captors surrounded them menacingly.

Suddenly the brothers caught sight of a transparent curtain near one end of the room. A figure was seated behind it, half turned toward them.

The boys gasped. "Dad!" they cried out, shocked by what they saw.

Mr. Hardy looked badly mauled and mistreated. His clothes were mussed and dirt-streaked. His head hung in an attitude of complete defeat!

The masked leader addressed the brothers. "You've been wondering about your father. Now you know. Mr. Hardy, your sons are here. Speak to them."

"Boys," he said, without moving, "you can't beat these men. Give up!"

Astonished, the boys tried to break loose and rush to him. But quickly the strong hands of their captors reached out and halted the brothers. They were whisked into an adjoining room and flung violently onto the floor.

Their blindfolds were retied and tape was fastened over their lips in place of the gags.

"That ought to hold you," the leader snarled as Frank and Joe struggled in vain, "until you go on your next trip."

The boys wondered what he meant, and an explanation was immediately forthcoming.

"We'll be back to put you on a freighter," he went on, "and when it reaches its destination, you won't be in a position to bother anybody!"

The door slammed and footfalls told the Hardys that the men had gone. After waiting to make sure that a guard had not been posted, they struggled against their bonds, grunting and panting behind their sealed lips. But the men had done their work well. The ropes would not budge an inch! Exhausted, they sprawled on the floor.

Suddenly Frank got an idea. "It might work," he told himself hopefully.

Crawling over to Joe, he raised himself erect, using his brother's body as a prop. Slipping his bound wrists over the doorknob, he wriggled his hands round and round.

Finally one of the bonds loosened, then another. Frank twisted his hands violently. The ropes slipped. He was free!

Quickly Frank ripped off the blindfold and the adhesive tape, then released his brother.

"Thank goodness!" Joe whispered. "Now to break out of here!"

Rubbing their chafed wrists, the boys surveyed the dingy little room. The only exit was the door. When it refused to open, Joe said:

"Come on. Let's crash it!"

Rearing back, they heaved against the door. Once, twice, then a loud splintering noise and the door gave way.

Crashing into the other room, the boys looked for their father. But he as well as the men had vanished!

"They've taken Dad with them!" Joe cried.

"Come on," Frank urged. "Let's get out of here. We have work to do to save him!"

Racing down the steps, the boys emerged into the street. They gazed around them.

"This place looks familiar," Frank said, then added excitedly as he saw a store sign, "We're in Southport!"

"Let's get to the police fast, Frank," Joe urged, "before those men get far away with Dad!"

"Hold on a minute!" Frank exclaimed, a strange look coming over his face. "There's something mighty queer about this whole deal. Before we see the police, I suggest that we get in touch with Mother and with Sam Radley."

"You suspect something?" Joe asked.

"I sure do. Something we can take care of better without the police."

CHAPTER XIX

Under the Whip

"THAT man we thought was Dad wasn't Dad at all," Frank told Joe.

"What!"

"Bet you anything! He'd have given us some sign."

"But it was his voice," Joe protested.

"That's the only part which puzzles me," Frank confessed. "But before we go to the police, let's check with Sam Radley and find out whether he's heard from Mr. Bryant."

"Good idea. But how about some food?"

"You find a cab and I'll grab some sandwiches."

"With what?" Joe asked. "They don't give food away free around here."

Frank realized ruefully that they did not have any money with them and knew no one in town but the police.

"I guess we'll have to go to them after all and borrow some money."

They walked to headquarters and told the story of their kidnaping. The captain said he would investigate the place at once. By the time the boys had washed, combed their hair, and brushed their clothes, the officers had returned. They reported that the kidnapers had helped themselves to a vacant apartment!

"So I'm sure they won't return," the captain commented, adding that Breck and York had not been seen in Southport.

The boys asked for a loan of ten dollars, then left. Munching sandwiches and drinking soda on their way in the cab, Frank and Joe pulled up at the Bayport Hospital. They were dismayed to be denied admittance.

"Visiting hours are nearly over," a nurse told them primly.

"But it's important that we see Mr. Sam Radley," Joe said. "He's a detective and—"

"All the more reason for leaving him alone," she broke in firmly. "He needs rest and quiet. There's only five minutes left. Come tomorrow if you like."

Disconsolately the brothers walked outside.

"This is a heck of a time to be thwarted on a case," Frank muttered.

"Say," Joe exclaimed, "I know another way to get upstairs—through the back way. Come on!"

Cutting around the hospital grounds, the boys reached a small doorway in the rear. It was one the interns used and was little known to the general public.

"Sh!" Joe whispered. "If that nurse catches us, the jig's up!" They found a flight of stairs and hurried up to the floor where Sam Radley's private room was located, then tiptoed down the corridor and entered 406.

The detective was lying in bed reading. He looked up over the top of the paper.

"Why, hello, Frank and Joe. Where'd you come from?" he asked in astonishment.

Frank held his fingers to his lips, signaling for silence.

"It's a long story and we have only four minutes," he replied quickly. He briefly outlined their adventures, ending with his suspicions about the man at Southport not being Mr. Hardy.

"You could be right," Sam conceded. "But I wouldn't worry about your father. Here's a wire from Mr. Bryant."

He picked up the telegram from his night table. As he handed it over, a bell rang, warning visitors to leave.

"Stop worrying about your boss," the message read.

"That practically proves the man in Southport wasn't Dad," Frank said.

"Not necessarily," Sam replied. "It's just possible

your father allowed himself to be captured on purpose to get closer to the gang and its operations."

"But why did he warn us to lay off?" Joe asked.

"For two reasons: so you wouldn't get hurt, and also so you wouldn't interfere with his own sleuthing."

"That might be, but I still don't believe the man we saw in Southport was Dad."

"I don't agree with you, Frank," his brother contradicted. "The gang could have had an actor pose to look like Dad. But I'm sure even an actor couldn't imitate his voice so perfectly."

Another gong sounded, and a nurse appeared in the doorway.

"Visitors must leave now," she said, and to be sure they did, the nurse waited until the boys bid Sam good night and hurried down the corridor.

As the brothers turned in the direction of their own home, Joe suddenly grinned. "Mother and Aunt Gertrude will certainly be surprised to see us. They think that we're still up in the mountains."

"We'd better ring the bell instead of using a key," Frank advised.

"Mine's up in Ramapan country, anyway," Joe said.

"Who's there?" a suspicious voice called from behind the door.

"It's Frank and Joe, Aunt Gertrude," Frank answered.

The door swung open wide. "Joe! Frank!" she cried. "What a surprise to see you! But I'm glad you're home. Your place is home, not gallivanting off to—"

"Wait a minute, Auntie," Frank interrupted. "We're not staying long."

"Who's there?" Mrs. Hardy asked, coming to the hallway. "My boys!" she exclaimed, hugging them. "How good to see you!"

The reason for their sudden appearance was soon told. The women's eyes widened in amazement, and they asked the boys to reconsider going back to the dangerous area.

"But we don't know what happened to Ted Whitestone!" Joe said. "He may be a prisoner."

"I understand," Mrs. Hardy replied with a smile. "How about telephoning to his father?"

"We'll do that, anyway," Frank said. "But if we're going to solve the Ramapan mystery, we must work before the Hunter's Moon is gone."

"Then you boys had better get some sleep and be on your way," their mother said understandingly.

When Frank talked to Chief Whitestone, the man said a search had already been instituted for all three boys. He was amazed to hear what had happened, and was glad that the Hardys had escaped. The chief said grimly he would notify the police about Smirkis and the other men and that efforts to find his son would be redoubled.

"We'll be back as soon as we can get there to help you," Frank promised.

"That's fine, but I'm afraid Ted is miles away by this time," his father said woefully.

Joe called the airport and learned that a plane which left Bayport at five in the morning stopped at Lantern Junction. He quickly made reservations.

Meanwhile, Frank had begun to worry about the safety of his mother and Aunt Gertrude. He was afraid that when the gang found out the boys had escaped they might come to the Hardy home and seek revenge.

"I'm going to ask Chief Collig to post plain-clothes men at the house day and night," he said, and dialed the police station.

Collig was not there, but he left the message with the sergeant who promised co-operation.

"A man will be here in a few minutes," Frank reported to his family.

He and Joe set an alarm clock and tumbled into bed. The next morning they found it hard to awaken when the buzzer sounded at four-fifteen, but they got up and dressed quickly. After kissing their mother good-by, the brothers quickly left the house. They stopped for a moment to talk with the police detective on guard, then started for the airport.

Arriving barely in time, the Hardys took their seats in the small plane that serviced the mountainous region of the Ramapan country. An hour later they landed near Lantern Junction and were driven to town. After a hearty breakfast at the Grand Hotel Frank and Joe set out once more for the Indian village.

"We'd better keep our eyes open for anybody lying in wait for us," Frank advised. "I'll lead off and look in front and to the right. Suppose you keep track of what's on our left and in back of us."

"Okay."

But they saw no one and reached the Ramapan village without incident. When Chief Whitestone opened the door, he grasped their hands eagerly.

"You're back! But there's no word of Ted! You have no idea where he might be?"

"I'm afraid, Chief Whitestone," Frank said, "that he's a prisoner of the people who are trying to get your land away from you."

The Indian stared unbelievingly. "You mean they're holding him as a hostage?"

"Probably."

"I had no idea what danger you'd get into when I asked you to find the deed," the chief said. "And my son, we've looked in vain for him so far. Chet and some of the villagers as well as the police are out now hunting for him. Have you anything to suggest?"

The boys said they were so sure that Smirkis was holding Ted prisoner that they should bend their efforts in that direction.

"Let's phone Mike right away," said Frank.

He dashed to the Indian chief's telephone. Seconds later he realized that the wire was dead.

"More of the gang's work," said Frank in disgust. "They cut the line!"

Joe suggested that the brothers hurry to town and tell their story to the police. Without waiting for Chet's return, the boys hurried back to Lantern Junction and went to headquarters.

"We think Ted was taken away by Smirkis," Joe said. "Can you tell us anything about his haunts so we can look for him too?"

Mike ran his fingers through his hair several times before replying. Suddenly he snapped his fingers.

"The cabin!" he exclaimed. "That's the place. It just came to me. Smirkis once had a hunting cabin in the woods. He sold it, but I'll bet that's where he's hiding."

The Hardys were on their feet in an instant. "Come on!" exclaimed Frank. "Let's have a look right away!"

The officer got his car and they drove a couple of miles out of town. Mike parked and they started off through a heavily overgrown area for Smirkis' hunting cabin.

After a twenty-minute trek Mike suddenly held up his hand and motioned them to be quiet.

"It's just through those trees," he said, pointing.

Treading carefully the three moved silently toward the cabin. There was no sign of life around the place.

Joe ducked down and moved to a spot underneath

a window. The others followed. Raising their heads, they peered inside the cabin.

In the dusky room they could see nothing at first, then suddenly each received a shock.

Ted Whitestone was trussed up and propped against the wall!

Smirkis was standing in front of him, a whip held menacingly in one hand.

"You'd better come clean!" he snarled at the boy. "If you don't, you'll get more of this whip!"

"You can't get me to talk by torture!" Ted answered defiantly, looking Smirkis squarely in the eye.

The onlookers could see several angry welts on the boy's cheeks.

"Where's that buried treasure?" Smirkis demanded.

"I don't know."

"What do you mean you don't know?" Smirkis snarled, using the whip on the boy's hands. "You know all right, but you and your father are trying to keep the treasure for yourselves!"

Mike signaled the Hardys. "Okay," he whispered. "It's time to move! Circle the cabin!"

The brothers took strategic positions so Smirkis could not escape. Then, with a tremendous crash, Mike assailed the door and burst into the room!

CHAPTER XX

A Wigwam Hide-out

THE POLICE officer dived for Smirkis. Though taken off guard the wily swindler was not to be caught so easily. He slashed his opponent with the whip, then leaped through a window.

But he was trapped. Frank and Joe converged on him from either side.

"Okay. I give up, but I can explain everything," Smirkis declared as they led him inside the cabin.

Meanwhile, Mike was releasing Ted from his bonds. The Hardys turned their prisoner over to the police officer and rushed up to Ted.

"It's sure good to see you fellows," the Indian boy said, chafing his wrists where the ropes had been fastened.

"Are you all right, Ted?" Frank asked.

"I guess you just got here in time," he replied soberly, feeling the welts on his face. They all turned their attention to Smirkis.

"You'd better come clean," Mike told him. "Who's paying you and what do they want?"

"I don't know," the man replied sullenly.

"You don't know, eh?" the officer said skeptically. "You mean you work for men you don't even know! You're not that dumb."

Smirkis hung his head. "Honest I don't know. What I mean is, a stranger hired me."

"But what was his name?"

"He didn't tell me his name. He just said, 'Call me Al. I'll pay you well.'"

"For what?"

"To do some spying for him."

"What kind of spying?"

"He told me to spy on the Ramapans. He said they had a fabulous buried treasure." Smirkis avoided the boys' eyes.

"A spy, eh?" Frank broke in. "Find out anything?"

"No," Smirkis muttered.

The Hardys wondered if he were telling the truth.

"Where is this Al now?" Joe asked.

The prisoner shrugged.

"Where did he stay when he was in town?" Mike prodded him.

Smirkis looked at his captors sheepishly. "I let him stay in this cabin. I knew the owner wouldn't come here. Al told me he couldn't afford to be seen in town."

"Wanted, eh?" the officer remarked.

"What did Al look like?" Frank asked.

"He's a dark, heavy-set man. About thirty-five, I'd say. He has a bad scar on the back of his right hand. Looks like a W."

"A W-shaped scar on the back of his hand!" Joe exclaimed. "Breck! Boy, does that explain a lot!"

"Good work!" the police officer said admiringly to the Hardys. "This Al or Breck—whatever his name is—we'll set a watch on this cabin, and if he shows up, we'll bring him in."

Mike took the prisoner back to town, and the boys set out for the Ramapan village.

"Did that guy talk to you all the time?" Frank asked Ted.

"No. He slept a lot, and once he went off for several hours."

"To cut the telephone line at your house," Joe deduced.

"At first he wasn't bad to me and gave me food regularly. But this morning he started whipping me 'cause I wouldn't talk."

Chief Whitestone was relieved to see his son, and Chet bubbled over with joy at seeing all three safe. Judging from the new notches in his belt, the stout youth had lost several pounds from worrying about his friends and from tramping about in the woods.

"This mystery gets more complicated," the chief remarked. "Since you've been gone, I've received a letter from that man you asked me about—Philip York."

"Philip York?" the Hardys chorused.

"He claims to be the grandson, by a former marriage, of the Amos York who once owned this land. You recall we bought it from his estate."

"What did Philip York want?" Frank asked.

"He says his father didn't get his share of the money when the property was sold."

"Has he any real claim?" Chet put in.

"If he has, we're in trouble," Chief Whitestone replied, "because all heirs have to be accounted for when any land is sold."

"Didn't the lawyers know about him?" Joe wanted to know.

"Philip York claims his father knew nothing about the deal. If that's true, then the sale of the property was illegal and the transaction has to be made all over again."

"Whew!" Joe whistled. "And you'd have to pay anything extra they might ask?"

"Yes," the chief said, frowning. "York claims he has half brothers and sisters to be paid in addition. They could insist we give them a small fortune to sign off. And we just haven't got the money."

There was silence for a few moments, then Chief Whitestone continued. "The second thing I'm worried about is a little closer to home."

"What is it?" Frank asked anxiously.

"Someone has been digging around the spot where we were looking for the buried treasure!"

"When did you discover it?" Joe questioned.

"I found bootmarks and freshly turned earth there this morning, which means someone must have been digging last night."

The boys gasped. "I wonder if the digger found anything?" Ted exclaimed.

Chief Whitestone tapped his pipe on the table, then replied, "It's hard to tell, Ted. Whoever it was dug quite deep, though. We can only hope he failed in his search."

"Father, we must find out whether he was successful!"

"But how?" Chief Whitestone asked.

Almost immediately Frank came up with a plan. "We'll fool him. We'll use a decoy."

"What kind of decoy?" Ted asked.

"The best decoy in the world," he told them. "The whole Ramapan tribe!"

"The whole tribe! Frank, you've got wheels in your head!" Chet exclaimed. "You just better forget this mystery for a while!"

Frank shook his head and smiled.

"Here's the idea—crazy or not, it might work. The Ramapans can put on their Hunter's Moon ceremonial dance this evening instead of waiting. Have it at some point a short distance from the crisscross shadow."

"I see," said Joe. "If the digger didn't find the treasure, he'll be back."

"Exactly. While everyone is watching the dance,

he'll count on being alone. But you and I, Joe, will keep watch by the wigwam."

"Great idea, Frank," Chief Whitestone responded, slapping the youth on the back. "I'll get the preparations for the ceremonial dance started right away."

"Say," remarked Chet eagerly, "that's really a corker of a plan after all, Frank!"

The Hardys became restless as they waited, but finally darkness fell and the brilliant Hunter's Moon rose like a flaming ball. Under its bright, glowing light the weird ceremony started.

First came the beat of the drums, beginning slowly, but growing more insistent. Then the dancers, dressed in war paint and feathers, started their elaborate rhythmical movements. They chanted, leaped, and twisted, as they circled the soaring flames of the great bonfire.

The dance soon got into full swing, with Indian faces reflecting the blaze of the fire and the drums pounding wildly. Although the boys found the strange ritual fascinating, Frank finally whispered to his brother:

"We'd better go. We have work to do at another place."

Walking stealthily they went straight to the place of the crisscross shadow. No one was around. They slipped inside the wigwam and waited.

Presently Joe peeked out of the opening. For a moment all he could see was the frozen ground and the dark forest trees, still in the silver moonlight. Then he gave a sudden start.

"A man's coming!" he reported excitedly. "Let's grab him!"

As the man came nearer, the boys rushed outside. At this very moment something whizzed over their heads. A second later a large dagger struck the back side of the wigwam!

CHAPTER XXI

A Moonlight Search

FRANK seized his brother by the shoulder and jerked him to the ground.

"That man's trying to kill us!"

Terrified, the boys waited, their faces pressed into the cold ground. Then they heard the sound of running footsteps.

Joe raised up. "I guess he's gone. Whew! That was a close shave!"

"Close is right," Frank agreed grimly.

"I thought knife throwing in Indian country had gone out of style years ago!" his brother remarked.

"Not when buried treasure is at stake, Joe. Well, we proved our point. The gang hasn't yet found the treasure!"

"And neither have we," Joe pointed out.

They walked back to the ceremonial dance, but found that the rite had been completed and the members of the tribe were returning home. Quickly the boys sought Chief Whitestone.

"There he is, Frank."

The tribe's leader was talking soberly with a group of elderly men. Joe caught the chief's eye and signaled that he wanted to see him. He came over in a few minutes.

"Anything happen?" the chief asked.

Briefly the boys recounted the experience with the knife thrower.

"I'll keep guards posted here day and night," the man said gravely.

The chief beckoned to a couple of sturdy young men, who had taken leading parts in the ceremony. After a few short commands from their leader, they stationed themselves near the wigwam.

"I can use a good night's sleep," said Chet, coming up to them. He yawned.

The brothers grinned. "All worn out from dancing, Chet?" Joe teased. "You should have been dodging daggers as we were."

"Wh-a-wh-what!" Hearing the story, he said, "Wow! We'd better cut out this night work."

"We'll cut it out for tonight, anyway," Frank agreed. "I'm going to phone Sam Radley to find out if he's heard anything from Dad and then hit the hay."

In the Indian chief's book-lined study, Frank picked up the phone which had been repaired earlier and gave the operator the number of the Bayport Hospital.

"Mr. Sam Radley, please," he said to the hospital operator. "What! He's disappeared! With a broken leg!"

Frank hung up and turned to the boys. "Sam vanished from the hospital very mysteriously this morning. Left money on the bureau for his bill. No one saw him leave."

The boys looked at one another in amazement. Then Joe said, "How'd he walk with his leg in a cast? Try his hotel. Maybe he's there."

But Sam was not at his hotel and the clerk there had not heard from him.

"Do you suppose," Frank mused slowly, "that his mysterious disappearance has anything to do with the saboteurs?"

"Maybe he's gone after them," Chet suggested.

"More likely the gang has taken him captive," Joe said worriedly.

The three boys sat lost in thought for several minutes, then Frank said, "I know somebody who might throw some light on his whereabouts."

"Who?"

"Jack Wayne. Maybe Jack took Sam on a secret plane flight!"

"You're right. Let's phone him."

Jack Wayne was a close friend of the Hardys. He owned a plane, and often piloted the boys, their father, or Sam on errands when speed and secrecy were needed to crack a case.

In a short time Frank was talking to Jack. "Have you seen Sam Radley?" he asked the young pilot.

"Why do you want to know?"

Frank explained.

"W-e-l-l," Jack began, as if reluctant to reply. "I don't know whether I should tell you or not, but I have seen Sam. Flew him on a secret mission to Chicago this afternoon."

"Did he give any details?" Frank wanted to know.

"Sam didn't volunteer much information, and he swore me to secrecy, Frank. All I can tell you is this: continue your investigations at the Ramapan village, and don't worry about a thing!"

Frank looked puzzled when he finished talking to Jack and repeated the conversation to his brother and Chet.

"Continue our work, eh?" Joe said, mulling over Jack's advice.

"But where?" Chet asked. "There's nothing to continue. We've dug at the crisscross shadow for the buried treasure, and didn't find it. All we have to show is a big pile of dirt!"

"We've sure gone deep enough," Joe declared. "You know what I think: that we haven't been digging at the right crisscross shadow!"

"You've hit the nail on the head." Frank thumped the arm of his chair. "There's only one thing to do.

Find the real crisscross shadow. We must do it to-night."

"You mean we aren't going to get any sleep?" Chet howled.

"You don't have to go," Frank told his plump friend. "But if we wait until tomorrow night, it may be cloudy. With the moon blotted out, we'll really be stuck."

"Count me in!" Chet exclaimed. "I can always catch up on lost sleep tomorrow. But wait a second, fellows."

He dashed up to his bedroom. Ted wanted to go on the search, but his father forbade this because of his exhausted condition.

In a few moments Chet reappeared.

"Good grief!" Joe howled in laughter.

Chet kept a straight face. He was dressed in an Indian costume—feathers, fringes, and paint, which he had borrowed from the chief's collection.

"If I'm going to find the tribe's buried treasure, I ought to be dressed for the part," he explained, and then grinned widely as he took off most of them.

"Okay, Chief Wallapatookunk. Let's step on it!"

Ted and Chief Whitestone helped the brothers in their preparations. Finally, equipped with hooks, picks, shovels, rope, and flashlights, the boys started off for the clearing where the wigwam stood. When they arrived, Frank surveyed the area in the moonlight.

"The crisscross shadow has to be around here somewhere," he stated firmly. "If it wasn't made by a wigwam's poles, then there must be another object which casts a shadow of the same type."

Frank pointed to the sheer side of the mountain that rose out of the clearing.

"Let's climb up there and have a look," he suggested. "We'll be able to see over a wider expanse from that height, and we may catch something we haven't noticed before."

They started the climb but ten minutes later paused for breath.

"Whew, this is tough going," Chet exclaimed, puffing as he clambered up the wooded mountainside.

"What? Big Chief having hard time," Joe needled as he boosted himself up another foot.

"Just keep at it," encouraged Frank.

"Worse'n football practice," Chet grunted in reply.

Picking their way carefully up the steep slope, they finally reached the top of the mountain. The boys paused to catch their breath as they surveyed the whole panorama.

Their eyes swept back and forth across the scenic view below them. Intently they took in every detail, seeking the sign of the buried treasure.

"Nothing here," Frank said. "Let's look on the other side of the mountain."

They walked across the level summit which was

"One misstep and we'd be goners." Chet shivered as he peered down.

"We've got to get down there somehow!" Frank said with determination. "The future of the Ramapan tribe depends on our getting the deed to their property! There's a narrow ledge just below us. If we could only—"

"Let's try a rope," Joe suggested, uncoiling one he was carrying over his shoulder.

He flung the end far out over the edge of the cliff. It wriggled down the stone face.

"No, it won't reach," he said. "Not by twelve feet."

He reeled in the rope slowly, and they moved to another spot. This time it fell only a few feet closer to the ledge. They walked on and presently came to a spot where the tossed coil apparently swung to the floor of the ledge, although from where they were standing the end of it was not visible.

"Now we're getting some place," Chet chortled excitedly.

"Quick! Tie the rope around a tree," Frank called out. "I'll go down first."

"Say, whose idea was this treasure hunt?" Chet objected. But as he gave a look downward, he added, "On the other hand, I'd hate to be selfish."

The Hardys grinned as Joe securely tied one end of the rope to a large tree trunk. Frank tested it to be sure it would hold, then, clutching the rope firmly, let himself over the edge of the cliff and hand over hand started his descent. The rough surface of the cliff ripped his clothes and scuffed his boots.

Reaching the place where he thought the ledge continued under a sharply jutting overhang, he was doomed to disappointment. Instead of a flat surface there was a pinnacle upon which it would be impossible to land.

"It's no use," he called up.

The climb back was more difficult. The rope creaked and Joe and Chet feared it might fray apart from the constant rubbing against the rocks and toss Frank into space. But he finally made it and was hauled up the last few feet.

"Chet," Frank said, "how about your going back and telling Chief Whitestone what we've found out? He'll certainly want to throw a guard around this place until proper equipment can be brought to get down there. Meanwhile, Joe and I'll keep watch."

"Wouldn't one of you rather go—and—and announce it yourself?" Chet asked. "I don't want all the glory."

"Or the wild animals or dagger throwers maybe?" Joe teased.

"I didn't say that," Chet hedged. "I'll go."

He immediately crossed to the wooded side of the mountain and began to climb down. Hindered by his bulky figure and heavy clothes he slipped and slid, making a great deal of noise.

"Golly," he said to himself, as he sat down un-expectedly, "it hurts more getting to the bottom than to the top!"

Rising, Chet started the trek through the woods. Suddenly he halted, for he had heard a sound in the brush. The palms of his hands turned clammy as he listened intently. But he did not hear the rustling again.

Shrugging his shoulders, though his heart was hammering, Chet walked on, trying to tread as noise-lessly as possible. In a moment he heard the sound once more. This time it was directly behind him!

As he swung around he was grasped roughly and thrown to the ground. A hand was clapped over his mouth. He struggled violently, but his efforts were futile.

His masked captors bound and gagged him, then carried him to a large tree.

"Okay," one of the attackers said gruffly. "You know what to do with this pest!"

"Yeah, but he weighs a ton," another protested as Chet was hoisted up to the first limb.

In a few minutes Chet was tied to the upper part of the tree trunk, out of sight of the ground.

"Next we'll take care of those meddling Hardy boys!" the leader declared in an ominous voice.

When Chet heard the man's words, he was terror-stricken. As the men moved off, he struggled to free himself, but he could not budge an inch. His heart sank as he realized that he was powerless to warn his friends.

In the meantime, Frank and Joe had found a spot some fifty feet farther along the mountain where they thought they could get down to the ledge.

"Let's try it!" Joe urged. "Maybe we can hop across from there to the side where the shadow is."

They tied the rope around a tree.

"My turn this time," Joe declared.

He went down carefully, landed on the narrow ledge, and calculated the distance to the other side. Would they dare risk it?

"Okay. I'll start down," Frank called.

When he was within eight feet of the ledge, he felt the rope quiver. He looked up. His blood froze.

High above him, silhouetted against the moonlit sky, a masked face peered down at him. Alongside it was a hand holding a knife.

"Frank!" Joe cried in horror. "Somebody's going to cut the rope!"

Frank reached out desperately to save himself, but it was too late. With a single swipe of the knife, the strands were severed.

Frank went tumbling through the air!

CHAPTER XXIII

A Perilous Ruse

With superhuman effort Joe Hardy braced himself and caught Frank as he came hurtling down the cliffside.

But for several moments it was nip and tuck between life and death as they swayed and teetered near the rim of the ledge. Then Frank was able to regain his own balance.

Prayerfully the brothers sat down, oblivious even of the taunts being called down by the man at the top of the cliff. But finally his raucous voice broke in on their thoughts.

"Now what are you guys going to do?" he snarled.

Another joined him and jeered at the boys, "You can't go down. You can't go up. You're trapped!"

Frank and Joe knew only too well that their enemies were right. Suddenly they realized that the voices sounded familiar.

"That's Breck!" Frank whispered excitedly.

"And York!" Joe added.

"Well, that definitely ties Dad's and our cases together!"

"You bet!"

"Guess we'll just have to sit it out until help comes," Frank said. "Chet ought to be back soon."

But as the minutes passed and none of their friends arrived, the Hardys began to grow uneasy.

"Maybe Chet was captured," Joe remarked apprehensively.

The thought sobered them still more. Waiting made them nervous and fidgety. Finally Frank stood up.

"As long as we're here, let's cross over to the other ledge and look for the hidden papers and the dagger," he suggested.

By inching along the narrow strip they came to a place where the leap across was not too hazardous. In a few moments they were on the other side and hurrying to the spot where they had seen the crisscross shadow.

"Those men on the top of the cliff may think we've escaped." Frank chuckled.

"Let 'em think so! We'll be well screened!"

Reaching the place where the two rock pinnacles were casting their crisscross shadow in the moonlight against the cliffside, the boys could now see a narrow opening just below it.

"The papers are probably hidden in here somewhere," Frank remarked.

They took out their flashlights. Shielding the
beams from any prying eyes above them, they began
to search. Frank suggested that Joe take the section
above their heads, while he surveyed the lower part.

Looking carefully, the two young detectives went
over every inch of the rocky surface. For several minutes there was only the sound of their boots scraping
the floor of the narrow opening. Then suddenly Joe
gave a low cry.

"I've found a box!"

He pulled the small rusty chest from a miniature
cave hidden among the rocks. Frank turned his flashlight on it.

After trying unsuccessfully to open the lock, Joe
finally pried off the lid. From inside gleamed a mil-
lion beams of light.

"The jeweled dagger!" Joe cried excitedly, picking up the fabulous weapon. The handle was studded
with rubies, diamonds, and emeralds.

"A regular pirate's treasure!" Frank exclaimed.
"I'd like to have known the Frenchman who owned
this!"

"The papers are here too," Joe said, digging down
for a yellowed bundle.

"See if the deed is there," Frank told his brother.

Joe opened a legal-looking document. He scanned
it rapidly.

"This is it, Frank. The deed to the Ramapans' land!"

Just then they heard voices.

"We'd better hide this again," Frank advised.

Joe reached up and replaced the chest. Then quickly the boys scrambled out to the ledge. As they hurried along toward where they had leaped, the voices grew louder.

"Frank! Look over there! They're coming down!" Joe cried.

Two men were dangling on a long rope almost across from where the boys were standing.

The Hardys' first thought was to jump over and try to overpower the men as they touched the ledge, but they realized that a fight on the ledge would mean destruction for all of them. Frank and Joe decided to wait and see what the men's intentions were.

"One of them's Breck!" Frank whispered.

"And York's with him."

The pair had removed their masks and were cautiously making their way down the face of the cliff. The brothers stood by, waiting tensely.

"Maybe they're going to bargain with us," Joe said hopefully.

Frank did not agree, but replied, "We've got to outwit them. Let's try stalling them off until help comes."

"How?"

"I'm thinking," his brother answered. "We might—"

He had no chance to finish his sentence, for at that moment Breck dropped onto the ledge, and his companion followed a moment later. They jumped the span and faced the Hardy's menacingly.

"Keep your distance, Wylie Breck!" Frank warned him.

The boys had their shoulders to the wall of the ledge, alert for any move their enemies might make.

"Don't worry. We're not going to touch you. We'll let starvation take care of that."

"What we want to know," the other man spoke up, "is where the treasure's buried." He guffawed. "You found the crisscross shadow for us."

"What treasure?" Frank asked in a surprised tone of voice.

"Don't give us that innocent stuff," Breck growled. "You know where it is and you're going to tell us. You'd better come clean."

"How about a little exchange of information?" Frank countered. "You give us some, we'll give you some in return."

Joe clutched his brother's arm. "You're not going to tell them, are you?" he whispered anxiously.

Frank pressed Joe's fingers in a signal to let him know that this was part of his plan.

"A deal, eh?" Breck sneered. "You Hardy boys want to make a deal when you're cornered? What's the game?" He turned to his companion. "What do you think?"

"Sure," the other replied. "What have we got to lose?"

"Okay. Shoot," Breck said to the boys.

"Tell us, then," Frank asked, "what are you really after?"

"Very simple," Breck replied. "I'm only helping Mr. York here regain his rightful inheritance."

"What inheritance do you mean?" Joe spoke up. "This land?"

"Yes. It rightfully belongs to him."

"And what's more, we don't intend to let Chief Whitestone produce any papers to disprove it," York chimed in.

"We were getting along fine until you young medlers came into the picture," Breck went on. "You almost ruined things for us, but now we've got you and your fat friend too."

"Chet Morton's been captured?" Frank cried.

"Yeah."

Joe moved forward. He wanted to choke this ruthless scoundrel. But Frank held him back.

"We warned you to lay off," Breck sneered. "But you didn't pay any attention. You thought you were smart detectives, but look where it got you."

The boys remained silent, seething as Breck recounted the story of the plot to deprive the Ramapans of their land, most of which the Hardys knew.

"Now, you've come to the end of the line," Breck said, his voice becoming cold as steel. "You and your father. He'll suffer plenty, too!"

"Where's Dad?" Frank cried.

"That you won't find out. And now how about your end of the bargain? Let's hear your story. Where's the treasure hidden?"

When the boys did not answer at once, he cried, "Come on! It's almost daybreak and we've got to clear out of here before it gets light!"

Joe looked at Frank, who was clenching his fists.

"You want the treasure, eh?" the older boy parried.

"Hurry up!"

"Walk along this ledge," Frank said. "You'll find a slab of rock sticking out. Turn in there and keep going. Feel around for more sharp pointed rocks and start counting. When you get to the twelfth one, reach up."

Joe could hardly keep his face straight. How plausible Frank's story sounded!

Joe looked at his brother proudly. The two men in their eagerness forgot to be cautious. While they followed directions, arguing all the way, the boys waited for them to get a good distance along before speaking.

In a moment the men were out of earshot. Frank whispered to Joe:

"The rope! Let's use it now!"

Swiftly and silently the brothers jumped to the

other ledge. They grasped the rope, and reeling it as they climbed, worked their way to the top of the cliff.

Suddenly there came a shout of anger from below. "Hey, you double crossers, come back!" It was Breck shouting.

As the boys scrambled to the top, Breck and York yelled curses from below.

"We've made it!" Joe exclaimed, throwing his leg over the top of the cliff and dragging himself up. Frank quickly followed.

"You have, eh?" a voice cried out.

The boys looked up. Three strange men, obviously armed, had them ambushed!

"If you value your lives, don't run!" one shouted.

The unequal struggle lasted only a minute. The boys were once more prisoners. Getting a close look at one of the trio, Joe whispered to Frank:

"Look at the one in the Indian suit! He's the man I shadowed that day I was attacked by Smirkis!"

"Shut up, you!" the man ordered.

A second one said, "You guys have given us a lot of trouble. We ought to drop you over the cliff. What say, gang?"

Meanwhile, the rope which was tied around a tree had been let down. At this moment Breck and York appeared at the rim. It was daybreak now and in the light the boys could see their angry faces plainly.

"You lied about the treasure!" Breck yelled. "We

don't go for things like that! Come on, York! We'll show them!"

He grasped Frank by the shoulder while York grabbed Joe. With the others helping, the boys were slowly but surely pushed toward the edge of the cliff!

CHAPTER XXIV

Mousetrapped

WHEN Frank and Joe were only twenty feet from the cliff, struggling with all their might against the men who were shoving them backward toward certain death, Frank suddenly shouted at the top of his lungs:

"Time out!"

He had caught sight of two figures racing toward them. Chet and Ted!

Chet had escaped from his enemies, they thought thankfully. But now in his desire to rescue the Hardys, he was running straight into danger.

At Frank's outcry Chet stopped short and grabbed Ted. He was not sure what Frank had meant by his signal call, but he interpreted it to mean that he should wait. Anxiously he and Ted slipped behind a boulder to await further instructions.

The brothers' assailants, surprised at Frank's strange words, halted also.

"What's the idea?" Breck demanded.

Frank looked him squarely in the eye. "If you still want that treasure, for Pete's sake don't push us over the cliff. You don't know where it is and we do."

"That's right, boss," another of the men said.

"They double-crossed us once. They'll do it again," Breck replied.

"We didn't double-cross you before," Frank said. "We just didn't tell you to go far enough. Listen. You have nothing to lose. We're still your prisoners."

Breck thought this over a moment. "What are you driving at?" he asked finally.

"We want to live," was the simple answer.

"I say give them a chance," York spoke up. "We want those papers. We can keep torturing these guys until they tell us where they are."

"Okay," Breck said. Turning to his henchmen, he added, "You stay here with these boys. If they give you any trouble, you know what to do! York and I will go down the cliff again." He glared at the boys. "You'd better be telling us the truth this time! Where's the treasure?"

Frank had a desperate plan in mind. He hoped it would work!

"Continue from where you were before. A few yards to your left you'll see a narrow opening in the rocks. Walk five feet in there, reach up above your head and you'll find a box."

The eyes of Breck and York gleamed with excitement. Quickly they began to descend the rope to the ledge below. The three men who stayed behind took positions in a triangular formation to guard the Hardys.

All this time Joe had been listening dumfounded to his brother. Like the other two boys, however, he had realized that the captain of the Bayport High team had some ruse he was trying to work. Watching Frank closely and waiting with every muscle tense for a signal, Joe was rewarded a moment later.

"34—86X!" Frank yelled.

The secret play! Chet's number was 34. The center poised for action!

"34—86X!" Frank shouted again.

"Hey, what's the—" the guard on Frank's left started to say.

He got no further. The four boys rushed at their enemies. Frank, veering to the left, tackled one guard, throwing him to the ground. Joe mowed down the man on his right in a flying leap.

Chet, running pell-mell, neatly cut off the third guard who had started to the aid of the man Frank had attacked.

Again the secret defensive play had worked!

With the assistance of Ted's strong arms and light-ning-like movements, the boys soon brought the fight to a close and disarmed the men. The tables had been turned. The captors were now the captives!

As soon as he dared leave, Frank hurried to the edge of the cliff and quickly pulled up the rope, to keep Breck and York below. Coming back to the others, he said tersely:

"Give me a hand tying these fellows up."

"We ought to take them to your father, Ted," Joe suggested.

"That won't be necessary. I'll summon help," the Indian youth answered.

Cupping his hands to his mouth, Ted gave a weird cry. *"Ee-ooo-ay! Ee-ooo-ay! Ee-ooo-ay!"*

"That's the Ramapans' war cry," he explained. "Listen!"

From the valley below came an answer. *"Ee-ooo-ay! Ee-ooo-ay! Ee-ooo-ay!"*

"Help will be here in a few minutes," Ted told them.

The captives, fearful of what the Indians' wrath might mete out in the form of punishment, fought like wildcats in a desperate battle to gain their freedom. But although they loosened their bonds, the boys quickly subdued them and wound the rope tighter about the men.

"Well, Chet," Joe said as they dropped to the ground to rest, "tell us who captured you and how you got away."

Chet pointed to the roped-up men, then told the story of his capture.

"Ted rescued me from the tree," he concluded. "I managed to get the gag out of my mouth and then started hollering."

"It was a good thing I heard you, Chet, before these men did." Ted grinned. "You certainly can yell, fellow!"

A few minutes later a band of eight Ramapans burst into view, ready for battle. They looked disappointed upon learning that their enemies already were prisoners. Ted asked six of the Indians to take the men to their village to await the police.

"You two stay here," he directed the others. "There are more of the gang below." He pointed over the cliff wall.

When the rope was removed from the prisoners, who were marched off, Frank lowered it over the rim.

"I forgot to tell you, Ted," he said, "that Breck and York will be bringing the dagger and the deed up with them."

"What!"

Frank explained the desperate chance he had taken, but there was only praise from the Indians for his action.

Joe, meanwhile, had been inching forward on his stomach until he came to the edge of the precipice. He peered over.

"They're coming!" he reported in a hoarse whisper. "Breck has the box tied to his belt!"

The impatient boys got set to grab York, who was in the lead. As his head appeared over the rim, they grasped him under the arms and yanked him up.

"Okay," he said cheerfully before he realized who

his assistants were. Then, seeing them, he yelled, "Breck, they're loose!"

Breck's head jerked upward. Catching sight of the boys, he instantly started climbing down the rope.

"Stop!" Ted cried.

"You'll never get me!" screamed Breck from ten feet below them.

Frank and Joe grabbed the rope and began pulling it up. The movement caused Breck to sway out into space. He glanced downward, and a sickened look crossed his face. Then his courage returned.

"Cut it out!" he shouted. "You've got me but you'll never use these papers!"

Holding on with one hand, he began unfastening the box from his belt.

"You can't do that!" Ted cried.

"Oh, no!" Breck sneered. "Watch me!"

At that instant the Hardys gave a powerful yank on the rope. With Chet guarding York to avoid a slip-up, the three Indians, holding hands, made a human chain. With one man grasping the tree, they strained forward. Ted leaned out over the cliff and snatched the box from Breck just as he was about to drop it.

"You fiends!" he screamed.

A moment later he reached the top of the cliff, too wrathful to speak further. He looked around wildly for his guards. Not seeing them, he turned to York. But York remained silent.

"Thanks for getting the treasure for us," Chet said, relieving the tension.

The men looked on sullenly as Ted opened the box. Nothing had been disturbed, and everyone gasped upon seeing the jeweled dagger.

"And the deed—it's here!" Ted exclaimed jubilantly. "Frank and Joe, you've saved the Ramapans' home for them!"

"We couldn't have done it without you and Chet," Frank replied.

"No, indeed," Joe agreed. "We sure were in a tight spot a few minutes ago."

"Let's get started for your home with these prisoners, Ted," Frank urged. "Joe and I still have work to do."

"You mean you haven't solved the whole mystery?" Ted asked, amazed.

"There's a friend of these men I'd like to talk to."

"Who's that?"

"Miles Kamp, the lawyer," Frank replied.

The boys' prisoners flinched. Breck broke his silence.

"He's too slick for you!" he boasted. "Kamp's one of this country's cleverest lawyers."

"For certain characters," Frank shot at him. "Get moving!"

The prisoners were marched off, surrounded by their bodyguard. When they reached Ted's house, Chief Whitestone was overwhelmed. After meeting his erstwhile enemies, and being presented with the box. the chief fervently shook hands with the Hardys and Chet.

"My gratitude can never be expressed," he said. "The Ramapans will always remember your fine and dangerous work to help them. By adoption I pronounce you Hardy boys members of the Ramapan tribe! I understand you, Chet, already have inherited an Indian title."

"That's right," Chet replied.

"This is a great honor," the Hardys said in unison and accepted their adoption with a bow.

State troopers, who had been summoned by Chief Whitestone, arrived soon afterward and took the five captives away. Then Joe went to the telephone and called Chief Collig in Bayport. He briefly told of the recent arrests and the officer shouted his congratulations into the phone.

"That's great work, boys."

"We want you to arrest Miles Kamp at once," Joe said.

There was a snort on the other end of the wire, followed by a long throat-clearing sound.

"Joe, I'm sorry to say Kamp gave us the slip," Collig confessed.

"What!"

"My men were covering him day and night as you and Frank wanted. Then, one evening, he just disappeared from his office like a puff of smoke."

"No clues?"

"None."

Disappointed, Joe hung up and reported the conversation to Frank. His brother jumped from his chair.

"Maybe we can find out something from Breck and York!" he cried.

Calling a hasty good-by to the Whitestones, the brothers dashed for the door.

"If you don't need me," Chet spoke up, "I think I'll stay here a little longer. I want to find out some more about Chief Wallapatookunk."

"Enjoy yourself!" Joe laughed.

Frank and Joe raced after the troopers and their prisoners and twenty minutes later caught up with them. The group paused while the boys questioned Breck and York. At first the men refused to give any help as to where the wily lawyer might be found.

"You want Kamp to defend you, don't you?" Frank asked. "How are you going to find him? He's not at his home or his office any more."

"The skunk! Why not?" York shouted.

"Well, where can we locate him?" Joe prodded.

Without stopping to analyze the situation, York burst out, "He'd better come across! I'm not going to take this rap without a fight! Tell him to come here! Look for him at his boathouse."

"Where is it?" Frank asked.

"He never told me. He said it was his special hide-out when he wanted to get away from people and work on a case. But I'm pretty sure it's somewhere in Southport."

The Hardys waited no longer. Turning in another direction, they hurried to Lantern Junction. There they learned that a plane for Bayport would stop in an hour at the near-by airport.

The boys spent most of the interim at the hotel, satisfying their appetites which had been neglected for all too many hours. Then they rode to the airport and boarded the plane.

Reaching Bayport, they taxied home to pick up their car. Mrs. Hardy and Aunt Gertrude greeted them in surprise. The women were thrilled to hear that Breck, York, and their henchmen had been captured but were dismayed to hear the boys were about to go after Kamp at his boathouse.

"Why don't you let the police do it?" Aunt Gertrude said. "I'll bet that Southport water front is full of all sorts of wicked people."

"We'll dodge 'em all," Joe said, grinning.

The brothers drove off, going as fast as the speed limit allowed. Reaching the Southport water front, they parked the car and started walking. The first quarter mile contained only large piers, the second quarter the tenement district the boys had visited before.

"I guess the private boathouses are all up farther," Frank remarked.

They plodded on. As they reached the area where private boats were kept, he and Joe began questioning all the fishermen and craft owners they met. First, the boys would ask them if they knew where Miles Kamp's boathouse was, then inquire if they had ever seen a short, heavy-jowled man who was very near-sighted. At last they were rewarded. One workman said that although he did not know the man's name he had seen a person near by who fitted the description.

"I've noticed him going in and out of that green boathouse with the apartment over the water," he said, pointing down the shore a short distance.

"Thanks."

The brothers hurried along the dirt roadway back of the boathouses. Coming to the green one, they paused.

"Look!" Joe whispered. "Inside on the window sill."

Frank turned. On it lay a pair of thick-lensed glasses.

"I guess this is it, all right!"

Suddenly a burly man appeared from a boardwalk running along the side of the apartment.

"What do you want?" he asked in a gruff voice.

"We want to see Miles Kamp," Frank said boldly.

"What for?"

"A message from Breck," Joe replied in a confidential whisper.

The other's eyes widened. "Okay. Didn't know you were friends of his." He stood aside to let them pass and indicated the door. "Go right in."

As Frank slowly turned the knob, the brothers exchanged glances.

This was the big test! Would they win or lose?

CHAPTER XXV

A Victory Feast

THE BOYS entered the room and found Kamp lying on a sofa. A quick glance around the grimy shack convinced them that the bombastic lawyer was alone.

"Who is it?" the man asked, rising to peer at them nearsightedly. He blinked several times, then reached for his glasses on the window sill, but Joe moved them out of his reach.

"Your game is up, Kamp," Frank declared grimly. "Your gang has been taken prisoner!"

"What are you talking about?" he cried.

"You'd better confess," Joe said as he bound the lawyer's wrists and ankles with ropes they had carried in their pockets. The boys were running no risks that Kamp might slip through their clutches this time.

"Help! Help!" he cried loudly.

The guard outside heard Kamp and rushed in.

"What are you guys up to—" the man began. Then, catching sight of Kamp's bound wrists, he roared with anger. "You've tricked me, you young—"

The Hardys leaped at him. Frank in a diving tackle grasped the guard's ankles and Joe seized him around the chest. In a moment he was their captive along with his boss.

Frank now picked up Kamp's horn-rimmed glasses and adjusted them over the lawyer's ears.

"The Hardy boys!" he screamed. "How did you— what—?" He turned pale.

"Tell your story," Frank invited. "What was your connection with Breck and York?"

Having recovered himself, the nearsighted lawyer looked at the brothers blandly. "I don't know what you're after," he said. "Why do you want to take me prisoner?"

"You know very well why," Joe countered. "What's your connection with York?"

"York?" Kamp asked. "You want to know about him? Well, why didn't you say so? I'll tell you what little I know. Take this rope off."

"Not yet. You talk."

"York came to me with a story about having been cheated out of some property rights by an illegal sale to the Ramapans. I thought he had a legitimate case, so I took it. There's nothing wrong with a lawyer taking a case, is there?"

"It depends on the client," Frank replied skeptically. "What's Breck's part in the case?"

"Breck? Why he works for me. Kind of an errand boy. I had him working on this case to help York. That's all."

"That's all, eh? We'll see about that!" A familiar voice came from the doorway.

All eyes turned to see who the speaker was, although the boys recognized the voice instantly.

"Dad!"

"Sam Radley!"

The boys rushed over to greet their father and his assistant, who was using crutches.

"What a relief to see you two!" cried Joe. "Dad, you don't look beat up. We were worried about you."

"I know you were, but I couldn't tell you anything." The famous detective smiled warmly at his sons. "I'm in pretty good health," he added, winking broadly.

"How'd you know where to find us?" Frank asked, knowing his father wanted the subject changed.

"We stopped off at the house, and your mother told us where you'd be, so we traced you here. And not a minute too soon, I see." He surveyed the two prisoners who glared at him.

Joe turned to Sam. "Say, why did you leave the hospital so quickly?" he asked.

"Because," Sam answered with a meaningful look at Kamp, "I had a little visit from a so-called bone surgeon. These crooks sure thought of every angle, all right!"

"You mean," Frank said, amazed, "that someone from the gang came to see you, disguised as a physician?"

"Exactly," Sam declared. "In that way he gained entrance to the hospital, having persuaded the authorities there that my doctor had asked him to examine my leg.

"It was a clever attempt at worming information from me about your father's work," the assistant detective went on. "But from his conversation, I soon knew he was no doctor. I managed to evade his questions so that he wouldn't suspect I was on to his game."

"No wonder you made such a fast exit," Frank put in.

"I had to get out of there pronto before the gang sent someone back to try more desperate means to make me talk," Sam continued. "With the help of my own doctor—I took him into my confidence—I was able to get some crutches and hobble away in time."

"Kamp was lying to you boys," Mr. Hardy said, as all eyes focused again on the glum-faced lawyer. "Want to tell the truth, Kamp, or shall I do it for you?"

The lawyer looked sullen. He did not reply.

"Don't believe a word of that fairy tale Kamp was

telling you, boys," Fenton Hardy began. "He's no small city lawyer. He's the legal brains of a gang of saboteurs that has been terrorizing the country from coast to coast! But no longer. They've been rounded up."

The boys grinned triumphantly. They had been right about a connection between their case and the one on which their father had been working.

"The gang wanted the Ramapans' property," the detective continued, "to carry out a great plan. It's so secluded it would have made a wonderful hiding place for big-time saboteurs."

"Kamp, you hired a man named York to help you," Mr. Hardy said, "but his real name is Philip Varry. He's a small-time crook."

Mr. Hardy paused to let this sink in. Then he went on:

"You got Varry to pose as Philip York, a missing heir to the Ramapan land."

Kamp studied the floor for a moment, then he raised his eyes.

"I might as well tell you everything. We planned to have Varry force a sale of the property," he said. "When Whitestone wouldn't sell, we had to take stronger measures.

"When we learned that the records had been burned and the Ramapans' deed was missing, I sent Varry up there to try to find the deed. Then you Hardy boys got involved in the case."

"Did you send us the threatening note?" Frank asked.

"Yes."

"And one of your men pushed us onto the railroad track?"

"That was our work. I had a friend of mine yell from the street to distract everyone's attention."

"How did you know where we were going?" Frank asked the lawyer.

"I had a man shadowing you boys," Kamp replied. "The morning you found the school closed he heard you talking about it. But we couldn't win.

"While Phil was in the Lantern Junction station, he stole a suitcase full of leather articles. He gave them to me, and when Breck came to make his report, I turned them over to him to use as a ruse to get into your house."

"So he did steal the key from the ring and hand it over to you," Joe said. "Where'd he hide it—in his mouth?"

"Yes, and gave the key to me at police headquarters."

"Why did you want to get into our house?" Frank asked.

"We hoped to steal the key to your father's filing cabinet. There were letters and other documents in there that the saboteurs wanted. We could have broken into the cabinet, of course, but that would have set the police on us at once."

Frank told his father about the trick that had been played on them, and how puzzled they were by the voice.

"I can explain that," Mr. Hardy said. "I was on the West Coast making an anticrime movie. Part of the recording was stolen."

"Did the record say something about 'You can't beat these men. Give up!' " Joe asked excitedly.

His father smiled. "Yes, it did. The whole record said, 'The American Law Enforcement Agencies are the best in the world. You can't beat these men. Give up. Go home to your local communities and forget the idea that crime pays!'

"I didn't know who had stolen the recording, but you've solved that mystery, boys. They played a vital part of the record to make you believe I was a captive. Thank goodness they didn't succeed in scaring you off the case!"

"Was it the man masquerading as you who made us think you were in two places at once?" Frank asked.

"Yes. When I heard that someone was getting into plants to be sabotaged, made up to look like me through the photograph the gang had stolen from our house, I went after him.

"I didn't want my whereabouts traced, so I swore the hotel clerk to secrecy, and also the detective you boys put on my trail. I just couldn't afford to let anyone know my plans," Fenton Hardy explained.

"We can discuss the case at home, boys. But right now we'd better turn our prisoners over to the police."

At dinner Mrs. Hardy and Aunt Gertrude listened eagerly to the windup of the mystery of the crisscross shadow.

"I told you right from the start Breck was a criminal!" Aunt Gertrude said smugly. "I've been working on that myself all this time."

She went for her purse and produced a clipping several years old.

"The newspaper found this for me," she said. "Breck's never been any good. Once he was sent to jail as a confidence man."

"Nice evidence," Joe said admiringly.

Miss Hardy was pleased by the compliment and was about to reply when the telephone rang. Frank answered. He listened a few moments, then, hanging up, he turned to the others:

"It was Chet. Joe, you and I are to go up to Lantern Junction tomorrow to testify against Breck and Varry."

Joe grinned. "Never a dull moment."

Phoning Jack Wayne, the boys made arrangements for him to fly them to Lantern Junction. The next morning when they arrived they went straight to court, where Chet met them. The hearing was in progress. Later the Hardys gave testimony which the prosecutor said would send the swindlers to prison for long terms. And their trial for sabotage was yet to come!

After the hearing, Ted Whitestone invited the Bayport High boys and Jack Wayne to a farewell dinner with the Ramapans. "A real Indian feast," he promised them.

Next day, as they gathered at the Whitestone house, he made an announcement.

"We understand Chet's great-grandfather, Ezekiel Morton, was an Indian agent here and was made honorary chief of the Pashunks who used to live near by. We Ramapans want to honor young Chief Wallapatookunk, which we believe means *Eat-a Whole-Moose*."

Everyone smiled.

"And now, Chet," Ted continued, "we hope you won't have any trouble imitating your great-grand-father."

A whole side of venison was carried in and set before Chet! Everyone in the room roared with laughter.

Frank and Joe were surrounded with gifts the Indians had presented in gratitude for their work in locating the deed and the jeweled dagger. The Hardys had never received a greater ovation for solving a mystery. But another was to come when they had concluded **THE YELLOW FEATHER MYSTERY.**

"Well, I guess it's back to the old dull school and

football for us now." Chet sighed as he finished a third helping of venison.

"Dull? Football? Remember our defensive play 86X," Joe reminded him.

"That play took us through an exciting adventure," Frank said. "Without it, the Ramapans might not be feasting us so happily tonight."